Evil Returns

John Sturgeon

Black Rose Writing | Texas

ISBN: 978-1-68513-118-0
PUBLISHED BY BLACK ROSE WRITING
www.blackrosewriting.com

Printed in the United States of America
Suggested Retail Price (SRP) $20.95

Evil Returns is printed in Palatino Linotype

*As a planet-friendly publisher, Black Rose Writing does its best to eliminate unnecessary waste to reduce paper usage and energy costs, while never compromising the reading experience. As a result, the final word count vs. page count may not meet common expectations.

Keep reading.
It's one of the only ways to get smarter these days.

Evil Returns

A Nice Rest Ends

Tomorrow is the last day of October, and I am about to return to work. I spent a very nice day walking through Grant Park; it was warm with blue skies. One or two puffy clouds drifted by. The lake was very calm. I knew in as little as a week the weather could change, and Chicago would be a slave to the cold of winter. It seemed impossible that that kind of weather was so close on such a nice day.

My shoulder was fully healed and so was I. I hadn't touched any booze or opium since the night of the shooting on the pier at Clark Street. Joan had nursed me back and from what I'd heard the Levee had behaved itself with no outrageous crimes that the regular crew couldn't manage. This helped lower my worrying. I had heard that all was well in the District. I had even spoken to Lieutenant Shipley, and he told me to take as much time to heal as I needed. They wanted me back, but not before I was one hundred percent ready.

Even without being shot, the last days in August were enough to send people over the edge. The two lady killers, Madeline Marsden, and Patricia Farmer had been dealt with. Madeline was in the girls' ward and Patricia was doing her time on a work farm in Kentucky. She may never be cured, but her time down there might break her a bit.

The bastard who took Danny O'Donnell and then shot me on the pier was never identified. There was no doubt that he had some connection to and was working in concert with Christian Hanson, but because I was able to kill the rat, we will never get any answers from him. Hanson, still not located, was around and always a threat, but we had to find him to do anything about it. Finding Hanson was always a challenge.

Another bastard, Rupert Finch, was back in town and had escaped any attempt at prosecution. He had hired a competent attorney who made it clear the Finch had nothing to do with the Price family murders or the murder of Billy Baxter. When we had dispatched Arnold Perry and his friend at their little house, we had failed to get admission that Finch had hired anyone to do his dirty work. Without any real proof, it was hard to pin anything on him, but he was undeniably someone to keep an eye on. I was convinced he was up to no good.

I mentioned how well Joan had taken care of me after the shooting. In a way, we had both taken care of each other. She had moved into my apartment and was off the street. She made me happy. She also informed me that she was about to make me a father, some months down the road. This may have been the reason for my long walk today. I had been a father once to two little children; I had been a husband. My former wife and children had all been killed in the Iroquois Theatre fire in 03. I can still see their fire blackened faces in the morgue down on Federal Street. I must say that I am more nervous about this news than I am about returning to the Levee District. I have little conscience in dealing with the Levee scum; I also know that I am frightened to death about being a father again. This is not something that I can fail at.

Chapter One

I hadn't been back at my desk for an hour when the call came in. The first hour of the day had been spent talking with everyone on the second floor, accomplishing very little. I was certain the next few hours would not be so mundane. A boy had been found, a black boy, hanging from an oak tree down in the Irish section of the southside. The boy's hands had been bound behind him; his ankles tied as well. Somebody stuffed an old rag in his mouth. The cops who were on site said the kid might be thirteen or fourteen.

I went looking for George Loftus to make the drive out to see the body, but he had left the building on another matter. Riley O'Donnell was my next choice and we were soon making the five mile drive to the scene of the crime.

"That goddamn Loftus late again?" Riley mumbled.

"What's that?" I said, thinking about the black boy. Riley didn't answer.

"Sometimes I hear some of these negroes get to starting some trouble down there. The Irish don't care for much of that trouble," Riley said. He was driving; a half burnt cigarette was hanging from his mouth.

"The kid was something like thirteen, Riley," I said. "Can you think of something that a kid that age could have done that would cause someone to hang him?"

Riley took a drag on the cigarette and tossed the butt out the window. He didn't look at me. "Maybe the kid stole something."

"Yeah, maybe. Maybe he stole a whole house. That would seem a big enough theft to get hung up in tree."

"I don't know, Patrick. I'm just thinking out loud."

"You ever think that somebody just strung this kid up because they didn't like him or the color of his skin?"

Riley's eyes opened wide. "Up here? That stuff only happens down south, you know, the Klan and those people. They are the ones that have done the lynching. That stuff doesn't happen here."

"It just seems awfully bad that somebody was so mad at this kid that they hanged him. Just a damn kid."

Riley didn't answer right away. "I guess we'll find out soon enough," he said.

• • •

Near 63rd Street there is a large section of town that is almost exclusively Irish. The houses are simple and crowded. As immigrants came into the city they would flock to this area of town. To the south end of what was known as Irishtown, the area butted up against a growing black neighborhood. It was no secret that the two cultures clashed on occasion. Something bothered me about this black kid. It really bothered me that he had been murdered, but what bothered me more was why.

We had been summoned to an open area of land with quite a few trees. It wasn't hard to find where we were supposed to be going. There was a group of maybe fifty people surrounding a large oak tree. Most of the people were white, but we did see a few blacks wandering about. At this time the crowd seemed relatively quiet; the main attraction was the boy seen dangling from the tree.

We got through the crowd without incident and found two street cops holding the gathering at bay. I wasn't sure what the crowd intended on doing, but the street guys were not letting anyone near the body.

"We're glad you two showed up," one of the cops said. He was big and round, his belly stretching his uniform. "We didn't know what to do?"

"You did good," I said. "Anybody say anything to you?"

"Not a damn thing. We were told there was a disturbance here. When we got here we found him." The cop pointed up at the hanging body.

Whoever pegged his age had it about right. I would have guessed early teens. The boy was kind of tall, skinny, wearing dungarees over a dirty shirt. He wasn't wearing shoes and there were none on the ground. The wind blew hard, a cold one from the north, and the boy at the end of the rope rotated. I got a good look at the other side of his face where a rag hung out of his mouth. My stomach soured.

"All of these people standing around here and nobody heard or saw anything," the cop said. "We asked loudly and no one said a word."

"Got a feeling these Micks don't care too much for the niggers," the other cop said. His name was Berger, a big German. I knew him a bit. He was a hard one.

"Watch who you're calling Micks, Berger," Riley said behind me.

"Don't mean nothing, Detective. I'm just saying."

"Well don't," Riley said.

"That's enough," I said. I faced the crowd. "Anyone one of you see or hear anything about what happened to this boy?"

For such a large group, there was near silence. If anybody did know something, they weren't going to tell us. "If nobody saw or heard anything then I suggest you all go home. You've seen the main attraction anyway. Before you go, though; if you do know something, it might be in your best interest to let us know kind of quickly. We'd like to find who did this."

There was more silence, a few grumbles, but nothing specific. The crowd began to disperse slowly. I could hear the hanging rope rubbing against the tree as the wind twirled the body.

"Let's get the coroner's van out here. We are going to have to go over to the negro section and see what we can find out about this kid."

•

We drove the auto east on 75th Street. I knew there was a section of this area where there were a number of stores that serviced the black people. The Irish section had seemed a little rundown. This section looked impoverished. It was so dismal it seemed void of color.

"How do these people live like this?" Riley asked.

"These people?" I said.

"You know what I mean. Looks like a slum."

I couldn't argue with him. The buildings looked old and tattered. Even the stores showed nothing that would attract you to them. The only word that came to mind was drab.

"You got a plan, Patrick?"

"Yep. I'm going to park this big automobile and step out and stand beside it. Seeing how we're the only two white guys in the neighborhood and we're both wearing suits, they'll know we're the cops. Someone, probably with knowledge of the dead boy, will come out and talk with us."

Before Riley could answer, I pulled the car over on the side of the street and stepped out of it. I closed my door and leaned against the vehicle. The wind blew hard and some pieces of old newspaper fluttered down the street. Riley stayed seated in the auto. No one else seemed to be walking about. The wind blew hard again. It was cold.

I was standing there for maybe seven, eight minutes when a big man came walking around the corner. He was a tall man and very thick through the chest. He was wearing old gray slacks and a black jacket. He wore an old watch cap. He came around my side of the car and sized me up. He was about ten feet away.

"See anything that interests you?" I asked. I heard Riley get out of the car and close his door.

The man smiled, no teeth showing. "Could only mean the cops have arrived when two white men in suits come down here."

"You got a name?" I asked.

"Uh huh. Sam is what I go by."

I nodded. "Well, Sam, we are down here looking for some information. More precisely we are looking for information about who that boy was that got hung in that tree near 63rd."

His face tightened. "We always tell our little ones to stay out of that Irish section. They don't like us black folks. I'm pretty sure that James heard that tale before."

"James?"

"James Jefferson. Good kid from a good family, only about fourteen. What could a kid like that do that would make somebody want to hang him?"

"That's what we're trying to find out. Can you tell me where the Jeffersons live?"

Now Sam laughed when I said that. "You mean to tell me that you white policemen are really going to try and find out who did that to James? Most of the time we get the feeling when one of us gets murdered that you white people just figure it's one less nigger to worry about."

The damn wind almost blew my hat off. I righted it on my head. "You see Sam, I've got a boss that sent me out on this case so I have to do what he says."

He crossed his thick arms over his chest and spit into the street.

"I also don't hate black people. Most of the ones I have met seem very nice, almost too friendly. I also don't care for murderers, especially of children. So if you don't mind, I'd like to know where the Jeffersons live so I can try and find the son of a bitch that strung up poor James."

Sam smiled and uncrossed his arms and told us how we could find the Jeffersons.

• • •

The Jefferson home looked more like a shack than anything. The word ramshackle came to mind. The place was small, wooden and dirty. The front door looked to be barely hanging on. There might have been grass in front of the place, once. Now the yard was a mixture of dirt and weeds.

Again, there were no neighbors present when we got out of the vehicle. It seemed when word got around that the cops were in town that could only mean trouble. I got the feeling that Sam might be right. They didn't think we were there to help find James' killer. We would only be there to cause them problems.

We walked up to the front of the place and I knocked on the injured door. It was made of cheap wood and popped open as soon as I hit it. The door opened about a foot; I announced who I was and walked into the house. Riley wasn't right behind me, but did follow me in.

The house seemed to be one small room. There were two beds, an old table with a couple of mismatched chairs, a rusted stove and sink, and a floor that sagged with every step. At the table sat a woman, maybe forty or so, and an older man with a thick gray beard. They looked at us like we were a continuation of the bad news that had hit their family that day.

"Mrs. Jefferson?" I asked.

"This is Amelia Jefferson," the man said. "I am Curtis Jefferson, her father."

I took another couple of steps into the room. It was mostly lit from the light outside. There was a dimness to the room. I could see the mother better, now. She might have been attractive once, but age and life had beaten her up. The fact that she had been crying for a while didn't help.

"We in some trouble?" Curtis Jefferson asked.

The question caught me a little off guard. "Why would you be in trouble?" I asked. "We are here to talk about James. We're trying to find out who did that to him."

"Like we would know?" Amelia spat out. "Who hangs a fourteen year old boy? He ain't done nothing."

I heard Riley grunt behind me. "I am terribly sorry for your loss," I said. "I am here to help, but I need to ask some questions."

"The police don't often come down here to help us," Curtis said.

I smiled. "Maybe things are changing."

He gave a short laugh. "Yeah. Now they are hanging black boys up here in the north."

I took a deep breath. "You have any idea why James was up there in Irishtown?"

Amelia let out a small sob and rubbed at her eyes with an old handkerchief. Curtis put his hand on her shoulder. He turned to us. "James would go up there early in the mornings to see if he could find stuff that people had thrown away. Most of it was just trash, but once in while he'd find something he could sell, make a little money for it."

"Was the boy stealing?" Riley said loudly.

Curtis fixed Riley with a hard stare. "There you go, Detective, accusin when you got no right to. James was no thief. He was a good boy. He searched the alleys behind the houses for trash. That was it. He was no thief."

I nodded. "He would go up there on his own?"

Amelia shook her head quickly from side to side; Curtis patted her back again. "He would get up early," he said, "and go up there on his own. Maybe gone an hour or two. We knew something was bad when he didn't come home today. We knew he'd found trouble."

"He never got in any trouble up there?" I asked

Curtis shrugged. "Maybe some of the whites yelled at him to get away or somethin like that, but no real trouble."

• • •

"That kid was up there stealing," Riley said. He was back driving the auto. A cigarette dangled from his mouth. "I'd bet a week's salary. That old man was just hiding what he knew was the truth."

"Could be," I said. "What the hell did he steal that someone decided to string him up?"

"Maybe the people got tired of this kid running around in back of their houses before daylight. Maybe they thought he was responsible for some other crimes in the neighborhood."

"Maybe," I said. "Maybe it's deeper than that. Maybe they didn't like the way he looked, the color of his skin."

Riley chuckled. "Maybe," he said.

"You don't care too much for the negroes, do you, Riley?"

He turned to stare at me. He took the cigarette out of his mouth and flicked it out the window. "When it comes right down to it, Patrick, I'd say no. I think they are dirty and lazy. I think they belong in the South. Look at the way they live, crammed into those dirty hovels. They'll do anything to get food. Like this kid, James. I think he went to steal something and got caught by the wrong guy. I'm not saying hanging is the right thing, but if the kid was stealing?"

I didn't say anything. What could I say? They black area was depressing, a little like the Irish area, but worse. I'd had trouble with the Irish before. They were a tough lot. The negroes hadn't bothered me. Not yet, at least. Somebody had hanged James Jefferson. That was a fact. Why and who were the questions I wanted to answer.

· · ·

The lobby in the 22nd Precinct was overly crowded when we returned. What we had on the death of James Jefferson was nothing, but a dead fourteen year old boy. Was James a thief or just a black boy in the wrong part of town? I shook my head as we walked into the lobby.

A number of people were standing in front of the main desk. The desk sergeant, Coogan, never a friendly sort, looked particularly agitated. This brought me a feeling of amusement. Coogan and I were never buddies. He looked at me and I gave him a friendly wave.

"They are looking for you, Moses," Coogan said.

I stopped in my tracks. "Who would they be, Coogan?"

He smiled. "It's a surprise. They are all in Conference Room 2."

"They need me?" Riley said.

"Just Detective Moses, Riley."

I made my way past the crowd and towards the conference rooms. I had no idea why I was wanted or what might be important. I had a feeling that this might take precedence over James Jefferson.

I opened the door to number two and walked in. The room was silent based on the four people that were sitting in there. Lieutenant Shipley sat at one end of the table; George Loftus was on his left. Sitting in the center of the table was the ferret faced, little alderman Hinky Dink Kenna. Behind him, standing, was the much bigger and louder Bathhouse John Coughlin, the other crooked alderman from the first ward. Coughlin fixed me with a stare when I entered the room.

"Glad you could make it in," Coughlin said.

"I had a pressing issue in Irishtown," I said. "I'm sure Lieutenant Shipley filled you in on this."

Shipley rolled his eyes. "The two aldermen have an issue of their own that they would like you to look into."

"It's an unbelievable mess, an atrocious abomination of the law," Coughlin said. His face was a glowing, bright red. Hinky Dink, unsmiling as always, nodded his head solemnly.

"Some whore burned up a brothel owner in his own bed," George said. He had lit a cigarette and took a long drag. He didn't look good. "The aldermen here are claiming it was a murder, but the poor hooker had her face blackened and lost two teeth due to the owner punching her out. Her claim is self-defense against further attacks. She is out on bail, represented by our good friend, Attorney Bradley Luke."

"That is complete bullshit," Coughlin stammered. "She murdered the poor man while he slept, burned him alive. I want you to look into what else she may have done, what her history is."

"He wasn't some angel," Shipley said.

I saw James Jefferson hanging from the twisting rope. Importance and priority were coming into play. "Who is the victim and who is the killer?"

"The brothel owner is Horace Butross. He owns, or did own, I should say, Lustland," George said.

"He was a good Democrat," Coughlin barked.

I didn't care what kind of politician he was. They all ended up under the title of scum. I didn't know anything about the man. Lustland was a higher- end place on Wabash. "The prostitute?"

"One Lucy VonMara," George said. He couldn't resist smiling. "Currently residing on 18th Street."

"A murderer," Coughlin said. Hinky Dink nodded.

I looked at Shipley. He frowned. "We'll look into it," I said.

•   •   •

When the two aldermen had left the building, Shipley told George and I to follow him up to his office on the second floor. He had us close the door once we were all in the small room. His tie was in its usual spot of being too tight at his neck; his face seemed a bright red.

"So what was with the body out In Irishtown?" he asked.

"Just to make things a little stranger than having Coughlin and Hinky Dink show up here, we are dealing with a lynching," I said.

"Moses, I'm not really in the mood for your humor this day. I'm afraid the aldermen have caused my stomach to broil," Shipley said.

"No humor intended, Lieutenant. Someone hanged a fourteen year old black boy from a tall oak tree. None of the Irish folks in the area knew much. The kid's name is James Jefferson. He was a bit of a junk collector. Seems somebody didn't like him poking around in their trash."

I saw Shipley swallow hard. "Fourteen you say?"

"That's what I've been told."

He grabbed his pencil. "I will pencil you and Riley to follow up on that one; you and George can go check on Lucy what's her name?"

"VonMara," George said.

"I don't think Riley should help me with James Jefferson," I said.

"And why is that, Moses?"

"During our initial investigation of the case, I became aware that Riley doesn't seem to care for the negroes."

"I don't have a problem with negroes," George said. "I actually don't care for the Irish very much."

Shipley smiled. I don't think I've ever seen him laugh. He wrote down something. "You two will look into both cases." He stopped and thought for a minute. "You don't see anything big coming out of this James Jefferson thing? Is there any way that this could lead to some civil unrest?"

I'd never considered that. The Irish weren't thrilled that the blacks were encroaching on their neighborhood; the blacks wouldn't like it if more lynchings took place. "Could happen, I suppose."

"Keep an eye on that," he said, "but first go check on our arsonist prostitute. I don't want the aldermen showing up here very soon."

•   •   •

At one time, Lustland was a very nice two-story house on the south end of the Levee. Now it was a nice brothel. I had heard they played it straight and didn't want their girls to cheat or rob the patrons, but I knew that even if they had rules, the whores always had their tricks.

None of the girls were present when George and I showed up at the place. The madam, a nice looking woman named Miss Booker, greeted us less than warmly until we showed our badges. Then she managed to turn on the charm.

"Obviously, due to the tragedy, we will not be open today," she said. "The girls are all in a state of shock. Mr. Butross was like a father figure to some of them."

"Probably not Miss VonMara," I said.

Her face looked like she had just eaten a bad lemon. "I had a bad feeling about that woman as soon as we took her in."

"Tell us what happened," George said.

"Mr. Butross had a suite on the second floor. He had retired for the evening, sometime after midnight. One of the girls came running downstairs around twelve-thirty. She said there was smoke coming from underneath the suite's door. With some of the girls and a few customer's help we were able to get the door open. Luckily, the fire was contained to the bed, which was completely in flames. We were able to get enough water up there to put it out. It was then that we found Mr. Butross."

"Can we take a look?" I asked.

She led us upstairs and along a long hall to a bedroom that had its door closed. She pushed the door open and let us into the suite. There was enough light in the room to see the damage; there was also the heavy smell of burnt linens, maybe a body, too. The bed, what was left of it, looked like a charred mess. The walls were covered in a film of smoke damage.

"I'm guessing that Mr. Butross was a pretty deep sleeper if he didn't know that someone had set him on fire?" I said.

"Mr. Butross has battled excessive alcohol use for some time," she said. "My guess is he was inebriated past the point of recognizing anything."

"Don't think I've ever been so drunk that I didn't know I was on fire," George said. He looked to be recovering from his own hangover.

"I find nothing here a laughing matter," she said.

George apologized quietly; I thought the remark had some humor in it. "How did you figure out that Lucy VonMara had started the fire?"

"Quite simply. One of the other girls found her later. She was crying hysterically. She also had burns on both hands. Apparently, she was not the most careful person when setting the fire."

"Any reason why you think Ms. VonMara would have done this?" I asked.

"Again, very simple. Lucy was not a favorite of Mr. Butross. I am sure she was jealous, obviously angry."

"That's it?" George said. "Butross did nothing to her?"

She provided George with a defiant look. "Mr. Butross never did anything to any of the girls that would warrant something like that."

We were back on the walk in front of Lustland looking for a carriage. The day was chilly.

"Think this Butross was the angel she painted him to be?" George asked.

"Doubt it, but there are a number of ways we can check."

"I guess we should speak with the arsonist and murderer."

"That would be next."

"Think we should talk to Lawyer Luke first?"

"What fun would that be?"

⁕ ⁕ ⁕

We found the house where Lucy VonMara was staying. It was a boarding house for women on 18th Street. It was a little better than a flop house, but not by much. I knew the place had residents who were mostly former prostitutes or drug addicts. Many would be both. We found that Lucy lived on the second floor, third door on the left. We hoped she was home.

Surprisingly, the door was opened after we knocked only once. We were greeted by a tall, bosomy redhead. She was dressed in a rather showy nightgown and robe. She would have been very pretty except for the black eye and swollen, split lip. She didn't smile.

"You Lucy VonMara?" I asked.

"I'm out on bail," she said. "You should talk with my attorney."

"Your attorney doesn't like us. You don't have to talk with us, but we may be able to help you," I said.

Now she laughed a bit. "Why would the cops want to help me?"

"Good question. There's no doubt you killed Butross, but our question is why? You say self-defense of some sort, but a few friends of his say it's a murder. We don't care for a few of his friends, so we want to make sure we're getting all the facts before we can determine the truth."

She cocked her head to one side and gave me an odd look; I knew she wasn't buying my whole story. "Come on in for a minute," she said.

Her little room wasn't much, a bed and a table where a wash basin sat. A small dresser was in the corner. "Welcome to my home," she said.

"Maybe you should decorate," George said. "Spruce the place up."

She smirked. "You're kind of cute, Detective, but, your attempt at humor is failing me."

"Don't mind him," I said. "He doesn't get out much."

"I get out enough," George said.

Lucy smiled. "I'm sure you want to hear all of the gory details on the night that Mr. Butross was killed by me?"

"That would be a good place to start."

"He treats all of the other girls pretty well. With me, it was quite the opposite. He treated me like a slave."

"That's a little harsh, isn't it?"

"I don't think so."

"Miss Booker says you killed him because you were jealous of the other girls."

"Miss Booker is a liar. I killed him because of this." She pointed to her face.

"Why don't you just tell us what happened?" I said.

She sighed heavily. "I know that Horace Butross was supposed to be some great man for the community, helping the poor and all of that. He may have done some good things, but he was far from good. It was his understanding that the girls in his employment were there to provide special services for him. You see, he was a short, fat, unattractive man. He was a lousy drunk. No woman with an ounce of brains would fall for that, even with his money."

"When you say special services, I assume you mean sex?" I said.

"Now I see how you became a detective," she said. "Of course it was sex, but not normal sex. I heard he made some of the girls do awful things."

I put up my hands. "Spare me the details. What about you?"

"My turn came the other night. I was called up to his suite. All he was wearing was his underwear. He told me what he wanted me to do for him. This is something I had never done before. I told him no. I told him I found him repugnant. That was when he hit me. The first punch was to my lip. It staggered me. Then he punched me in the eye. I fell on the floor and he kicked me several times. I thought I was going to pass out. He stopped his attack and told me to get the hell out of his room.

"I made it back to my room. My lip was bleeding and I was coughing up some blood. Two teeth were gone. I was dizzy, but I was also furious. I knew the bastard was a drinker. He was drunk when I saw him. I knew he went to bed early, passing out from the whiskey. I waited a bit, maybe an hour. My plan was clear. I knew where they kept the kerosene for the lamps. I got it and returned to his suite. Like I said, he was out, snoring loudly. He never heard me or felt a thing when I doused him. The bed and him lit up like a torch. I got a couple of burns on my hands. I went back in my room until the cops came and got me."

"I understand why you killed him, but the whole self-defense thing might be a little weak," I said.

"There have been girls that have said no before, but they have been called back to his suite. Everyone eventually breaks, I'm told. I had no desire to ever break or submit to that pig. I knew he would beat me again. I took the stance that I needed to defend myself."

"He's hit other girls before?" George said.

"I heard yes, but none that are still with that house."

"But you can find them if we need to talk with them?" I said.

She shook her head. "I doubt it. I didn't know them, but I heard what had happened."

George shook his head. "That might be a little thin."

She crossed her arms across her chest. "My lawyer, Mr. Luke, doesn't think so."

"I wouldn't think he would," I said.

•   •   •

We waited in the cold for another carriage. I wanted to get back to see my friend Sam again about James Jefferson. We would need a vehicle for that little trip so back to the precinct we were headed.

"What do you think of Lucy?" George asked.

"Kind of liked her. She's smart, but I'm not sure how a jury sees her story. Yeah, Butross beat her, but she had time to plan and execute his death. That's murder in my book."

"Bastard sounds like he might have deserved it," he said. "I liked her; she was prettier than I thought she'd be. I thought she was funny."

"Don't like her too much. She still killed the guy. Like all of these damn cases, we only have parts of the story.'

"You really think we should head back out to the black section right now?"

"I do. When I talked to James Jefferson's mother and grandfather, I got the feeling they were holding something back from me. I'm hoping my new friend Sam can help us out."

•   •   •

His full name was Sam Fuller. He had given me his address before we had left him that morning. His house, like so many in the neighborhood, was small and needed repair, but it looked clean. Sam looked surprised when we knocked on the door and he saw who his visitors were.

"Detective Moses, I didn't expect to see you back here so soon," he said. He was standing in the doorway, preventing any view of the inside.

"Do you mean you didn't think we'd come back at all?" I asked.

He took a deep breath, his chest and arms swelling under his stained work shirt. "Like I said earlier, black boy dies and no one in the police department cares."

"You didn't believe me when I told you I cared?"

He smiled. "Come on in, out of the cold."

His house was a little bigger than the Jeffersons' and it was cleaner. His wife, a pretty woman, was sitting at a table with two children. They were eating stew or soup out of a bowl. They all glanced at the two white cops who came into their house, but none of them said anything. We were not introduced.

"So, you did come back," he said. "What more can I do for you?"

"When I was with the Jeffersons this morning, I got the feeling they weren't telling me the whole story. I felt they were leaving something out."

"What did they tell you?"

"That James used to go into Irishtown looking for junk that he could possibly keep and sell."

"That's what the boy did. He was a scavenger. Sometimes he would find some real good things. Other times, nothing."

"But he wasn't a thief?"

"James wasn't a thief. He was a good boy, trying to help his family. His daddy left them a long time ago, just his mama and grandpa. Whatever he was able to sell he would give to them."

"And you never heard anything about him being accused of stealing?" George said.

Sam looked at George and then back at me. "You seem to have found another partner. The one you had this morning didn't seem to care for the color of my skin."

"It doesn't bother me," George said.

"The answer is no, detectives. I never heard a thing about James stealing anything. If you want my opinion this is just another of those cases like we'd get down south. Makes me think of the Klan, going around hanging black men from trees. Were they all stealing? No. Those men were just killed because of the color of their skin."

"And no reason to think that James' mom and grandpa would withhold anything from their story they told."

"I can't think of anything, Detective. I honestly can't think of anything."

·   ·   ·

In a bit of irony, Joan had managed to secure work as a clerk in the great Marshall Field's store on State Street. I don't believe that she knew anything about my past employer and I didn't mention it. She worked from nine in the morning until six at night. When she returned to my apartment, she was tired from the day and her condition, but she still made a nice dinner. Tonight it was a chicken with potatoes and vegetables. The meal reminded me of the food I'd eaten over the years at Cooper's, but it had something Cooper's didn't, taste. There also wasn't an overindulgence in whiskey. I was grateful for both differences.

"You look very tired," I said.

She smiled at me as she was chewing her food. She swallowed. "Long day on your feet," she said. "Not always the friendliest customers, either."

"But the Customer is Always Right," I said parroting Field's slogan.

"That, Patrick Moses, is a crock of shit."

I laughed and felt how lucky I was at the moment.

"And how was your day, Detective?" she asked.

"No unruly customers," I said, "but somebody hanged a fourteen year old black boy over in Irishtown. I didn't even have that much time to look into it before we had to go over to Lustland to see about an owner who'd been torched in his own bed by one of the girls."

"Lustland? Nice place if I recall. She burnt him to death in his own bed?"

"No lie. Apparently, she said, he beat her up first. She paid him back in case he tried again with her. She's claiming self-defense. The state says she murdered him."

"Who's him?"

"Horace Butross. Know of him?"

She shrugged. "Not at all. What's the girl's name?"

"Lucy VonMara."

She thought for a moment. "Sounds familiar but can't seem to place her."

"Well, there are quite a few girls on the street."

She pointed her fork at me. "More and more each day. What about the black boy, hanged you said?"

"Just like in Mississippi. His people say he went into Irishtown looking for rubbish he could sell. More than likely he got strung up because somebody thought he was stealing something."

"Must have been something awfully big to get hanged. Doesn't matter. The kid was only fourteen, a black kid. The department going to give the investigation the whole treatment?"

"Maybe not the department, but I am."

She looked at me and smiled. She placed her hand on top of mine. "I never doubted that you wouldn't. I just wasn't sure how much the Chicago Police Department would care about some dead black kid."

Chapter Two

I hadn't seen the prosecutor Jeremiah Higgins since we had rerouted the murderer Patricia Farmer from her cushy girl's school to a work farm in Kentucky. I wasn't sure how he would greet me, but when he looked up and saw me a smile crossed his chubby face.

"I see that your wounds have healed," he said.

"All ready to serve this fine city and its citizens," I said.

"Come on in an have a seat, Patrick."

I took the only chair that didn't have papers and files on it. I noticed that Jeremiah's desk was covered with a lot of the same detritus; he was looking at me, adjusting his bow tie. "Are you looking for legal advice?" he asked.

"Should I be?"

"When I heard that Patricia Farmer disappeared, for some reason your name popped into my head."

"I heard that, too. She is a very smart and cunning girl."

Another smile. "Well, if it's not that case, why have you paid me this visit?"

"I'm interested in Horace Butross, formerly the owner of Lustland."

"Ah yes, the brothel owner fried by one of his prostitutes in his own bed."

"That would be the man."

Jeremiah leaned back in his chair, his belly stretching his too tight vest. "There is no doubt that the prostitute, Lucy VonMara, killed Butross. What is questionable is her claim that he beat her and she killed him in self-defense against further attacks."

"But the judge let her out on bail."

"He did. She was able to post bail and hired our old friend, Bradley Luke, to represent her. When she showed up in court she was sporting a black eye and a puffed up, split lip. The judge was moved by this and let her out."

"Maybe he was a former client?"

"In this town, you never know."

"How do you think a jury will react to her story?"

"A woman, even a prostitute, beaten by a man and then kills him, maybe gets some understanding, but Butross supposedly did a lot of good for the community, so who knows. What's your interest in this? She has already been arraigned."

"Our two aldermen came to the precinct and painted Butross as a saint. They just wanted us to look further into things to make sure that the prosecution of the case is solid."

"But you have doubts?"

"I got to meet Lucy VonMara. I kind of liked her and found her story believable. I'm just looking at it from all angles. I also have this feeling that if Butross was friends with Coughlin and Kenna, he might have been a bit of a scoundrel himself."

"Don't know. The man had no record of any type that we could find. I never heard of him until Lucy set him on fire. I'm thinking the self-defense thing is what needs to be looked into."

"He did hit her a couple of times."

"I'm not sure that gives her the right to torch him."

. . .

As I walked up the street towards the precinct building, a huge wind came howling off the lake and almost took my hat off. I had my head down against the cold as I made me way up the stairs. I almost ran into Father Richard Corcoran who was waiting at the top of the steps.

"Father Corcoran," I said.

"Hello Patrick," he said. "I checked inside, but they said you should be along any minute."

Corcoran was a younger man, tall, thin with red hair. He had come into Holy Trinity after I had left. I didn't know him well and from what I remember hearing about him wasn't bad. "You could have waited in there. It's kind of cold out here."

"I have a matter that I wish to discuss with you privately."

"A police matter?"

He shook his head. "I would prefer that you and I discuss it first. I'm not sure."

I became aware of how worried he looked. "Tell me what the problem is."

Corcoran looked around us to make sure no one was listening. "We have a young girl, Rebecca Tilson, who has been with us a while. She is only fifteen years old." He stopped and looked about again.

"What happened to her?"

"That's just it. We don't know, but she has gone missing. She was gone from the orphanage two days ago. No one has seen her."

"Just gone?"

"Two days ago. Her bed had been slept in, but she was nowhere to be seen. I checked with some of the girls who are her friends and they know nothing about it. They are all shocked and worried about her."

I thought about this for a minute. I had two cases that were very fresh. A missing persons case could be handled by anyone. I also had to take into consideration that Rebecca Tilson was an orphan and sometimes they just took off. "I think the best course here would be for you to file a report and we can get somebody to look into Rebecca. I think that's the best thing to do."

Corcoran grabbed my arm and looked squarely into my eyes. "I am very worried, Patrick. Rebecca is a good girl. This is completely out of character for her. I am also worried about what the Diocese would do if they found out. Also, if word got to the papers it could be very embarrassing. As a favor, I am asking that you look into it without going through the proper channels."

I could see the worry and fear on his face. Maybe something truly evil had happened to Rebecca. I felt my resistance give way. "Let me look into it."

• • •

I hadn't seen Harold Pinter since I had been back. I went downstairs to visit him in his little lab. Harold was seated at his desk, hands behind his head, looking up at the ceiling. He didn't even hear me as I entered his space.

"Anything interesting up there?" I asked.

He turned his gaze to me and sat up straight in his chair. "Oh, hello Patrick. I heard you had returned to work. I was wondering when you'd come by to say hello."

"I would have been by sooner, but two murders seem to have taken up most of my time."

"James Jefferson being one of those."

"Yes. James is the one I'm most interested in right now, although the dead brothel owner has my attention as well."

Harold nodded and pushed his glasses back up on his nose. "James is the one that you caught me thinking about."

"Any revelations?"

"No. More of a thought. It is amazing to me that we solve crimes in and around the Levee, extinguishing a bit of evil, but evil always seems to return."

"If there were no evil what would I do?"

"Perhaps be saner."

"Questionable," I said. "Nothing scientific you can tell me about James?"

"Oh, sure there is. There is always science. The first thing we have is the cause of death. Whatever he dropped off of, the fall broke his neck. This would have been enough to kill him. If not that than asphyxiation. I also noticed that his body showed no defensive wounds; James did not fight whoever did this too him."

"Is that important?"

"Not really, but it is almost as if he submitted to his assailants, gave up."

"Anything unusual that you saw?"

"Only the rope that was used to hang him. It was with the body at the morgue."

"What was unusual about the rope?"

"If I had to guess, I would say that this was the first time that this section of rope had been used. The rope was in pristine shape; I think it was brand new."

"Why would somebody use a brand new length of rope to hang this boy?"

"There are two reasons that I can think of. The person that did this had the rope and just didn't have any use for it before or their sole intention when they bought the rope was to use it for the hanging."

I rubbed my chin, thinking. "Nothing special about this piece of rope."

"Nothing. You could probably buy it at a dozen or so places that sell rope."

"Harold, you are not giving me much to pursue this killer."

He smiled. "Sometimes it is up to the detectives to figure these things out."

I laughed. "Most of the time we need to be a little lucky."

"By the way," he said, his face lighting up. "Congratulations, I heard you are about to become a father."

I doubted that Harold knew about my earlier marriage and children. "That is the truth."

"A special time and you are lucky to have a girl like Joan. All men deserve someone like her."

Harold was right. Joan was special and I was lucky to have her in my life.

•   •   •

When I came upstairs after seeing Harold I found George Loftus at his desk. The look on his face was one of annoyance and bewilderment. There was an older woman, gray haired, sitting in a chair next to George. I could see that she was talking quickly and motioning just as quickly with her hands. When George saw me he waved me over.

When I came up to the desk, the woman stopped speaking and looked embarrassed like I had interrupted a private discussion. "Who's your friend?" I asked.

George checked his notes. "This is Margaret Culhane. She just got here a few minutes ago. She wanted the detective in charge of the James Jefferson case. No one knew where you were so they gave her to me."

I extended my hand. "Miss Culhane," I said. "I am Patrick Moses. I am in charge of the Jefferson case."

"It's Mrs. Culhane," she said. "I have a husband Michael. He would not be happy if he knew I was here."

I placed her at somewhere around fifty. She had the pale Irish face with clear blue eyes that were behind round glasses. "Why would Michael not be happy if you were here?"

"He would not be happy that I was here talking about the black boy that was hung near the park. He told me quite loudly that it was none of our business. He told me that the black boy should not have been in our neighborhood." She spoke very clearly with a strong accent.

I pulled up another chair and sat in it. "Does Michael have some knowledge into who did that to James Jefferson? When you say that he told you that the black boy shouldn't be in your neighborhood, do you mean he doesn't like the blacks."

She shook her head. "Nothing like that. He couldn't care one way or another. He just thought the boy was inviting trouble by coming around us, so many Irish."

"I can't argue with him about that," I said. "Why have you come to see us this morning, Mrs. Culhane?"

"As I said, we don't mind the black people. They don't bother us and seem to be nice. You see, we are Catholics. We wish no harm or bad to come to anyone. That boy was so young, it made me sick. I have two sons, older, and I can't imagine what that mother feels today."

"Yes, mam," I said. "She is deeply sorrowed."

Margaret Culhane made the sign of the cross. "I'm not sure, but I may have an idea who carried out this awful sin." She stopped to look around the room. It was quiet except for us.

"What kind of idea?"

"There is a store owner, Bucky O'Neil, who comes to our church. He complains loudly about the blacks coming into his store and trying to steal. He claims openly that they are sinners, thieves and plague spreaders. He doesn't want them in his store because they are dirty and they smell. He tries to keep them out."

"I see," I said. "What kind of store does Mr. O'Neil run?"

"It is a general store on Sixty-seventh Street. Can't miss it. Has a big sign over the door that says O'Neil's."

"They would sell rope," I said out loud.

She looked perplexed for a moment. "Of course they sell rope."

• • •

Margaret Culhane's description of the sign over O'Neil's wasn't inaccurate. The sign ran the whole length of the front of the store and was painted a bright green. There were shamrocks present all over the sign. George and I entered the store which was doing a brisk business. We asked a clerk where we could find Bucky O'Neil and were told he was in his office in the back of the store.

Bucky O'Neil was a big man, well over six feet tall. Even as he sat in the chair behind his desk we could make out his equally large belly. His face was pale with thin red lines crossing a nose that had a red bump on the end of it. His reddish hair was thinning. He grunted when we showed him our badges.

"What the hell do you two want?" he asked.

"Watch your mouth, Bucky," George said.

"I haven't done anything that would require the cops to come in and roust me."

"Who's rousting you?" I said. "We just want to talk with you and ask a few questions."

He pointed to the piles of paper on his desk. "Ask away. As you can see, I'm going to be here a while."

I didn't like the man already. "You aware of the black boy that was hanged near the park yesterday?"

His smirk told me what he thought of the question. "Have to be dead to not know about it."

I laughed. "I guess. What do you think?"

"What do I think? I think the kid got caught stealing something and somebody made him pay for it. Probably about time."

"There a lot of theft going on around here?"

Now Bucky laughed. "Since the niggers got here, yeah. Those people come into our neighborhood and will steal anything that's not nailed down. Worse than the mice and rats that get into the store."

"I don't follow you on that," I said.

"It's not just that they steal, but they are dirty, they spread disease. I don't allow them in the store."

"I see. Any idea who might have strung that boy up."

"Not one," he said quickly. "Look, I know this was just some kid, but maybe it's a lesson. Stay over there where you belong and maybe nothing like this happens. Our people know how to stay away from the niggers. We don't go over there. It's just a fucking tenement anyway. Everybody is in need of something over there. That's why they come over here and steal."

"You sell rope here?" George asked suddenly.

"Of course I sell rope," Bucky said. "I sell any length and width you could be looking for."

"That's good," I said. "You have any records about who would have bought some rope in the past few weeks? The rope used in the hanging was brand new."

Bucky laughed again. "Sure, I got records, but it would take me a while to go through what people buy. I could ask the clerks, but this is a busy store. I doubt anyone would remember one sale that included rope."

"You talk to a lot of your customers?"

"Of course, except when I'm in here doing paperwork. I talk with people all the time."

"And nobody sticks out as being particularly upset about the blacks and the stealing?"

He glared at me. "Detective, this is a big problem. It effects everyone down here. It upsets us all. Somebody had just had enough. Maybe it wouldn't have happened if you cops had done more."

"What the hell you mean by that?" George asked.

"You cops don't even want to go over there to see what they're up to. You don't see what vile pigs they are. You see that and wonder why they steal. It's obvious. It's a big problem, but the police are no help. Whoever hung that boy decided to deal out justice on his own."

We were driving back to the precinct, both of us a little deflated by our conversation with Bucky O'Neil. "What do you think, George?"

"I think that man was an asshole."

"Besides that?"

"He has enough anger and dislike in him for the negroes to put him on a list of suspects, but if what he says is true, there might be a lot of suspects."

"I wonder if Shipley might be right. It sounds like the kettle is overboiling down there. There could be some civil unrest."

"Let's worry about the murder, Patrick. The city can handle the riots."

.   .   .

We stopped by Lustland on our way back to the Levee. It was still early enough in the day where the girls wouldn't be busy and tied up with customers. Miss Booker, the madam, was pleasant enough and agreed to gather the girls who were in the house when Horace Butross had been burned to death. There were only three girls present and Miss Booker gathered them in the parlor.

Like most prostitutes, the three women looked tired. None of them had dressed in their nighttime fashion; all were wearing some sort of robe. Two had not applied much make-up or if they did it hadn't worked.

"I want to thank you ladies for taking the time to talk with us," I said. "We know this is the time that you get your rest."

This little comment did nothing to increase their participation. Most of them had probably dealt with the cops at some time and it probably had not been a great experience.

"We're here to try and figure out what happened between Mr. Butross and Miss VonMara," I said.

"The bitch cooked him in his own bed," a bosomy blonde said.

I smiled. "That is not disputed. What we want to know is what led up to that altercation?"

"She was crying and said that Horace had beaten her up," a small girl with muted brown hair said.

"Did Horace Butross ever beat any of you up?" I asked.

"Or make you do something you didn't want to do?" George added.

All three of the women shook their heads no, but they weren't looking us in the eye when they did so. "Did you all engage in sexual activities with Mr. Butross?"

"We liked our jobs," the blonde said. "Sleeping with one more man wasn't going to change things for me."

"It sounds like you might not believe that Mr. Butross beat up Lucy VonMara," I said.

The brunette in the middle of the group cleared her throat loudly. She was the oldest of the group, but maybe the prettiest. "Horace was harmless. We just looked at his requests to have sex with him as part of the job. He didn't harm any of us."

"But I asked about Lucy. Could he have harmed her?"

"Look, Detective," the blonde said. "Lucy had a smart mouth. Maybe she said something to Horace that upset him. Maybe that's what got her slapped a bit."

"And do you think that's okay for Butross to do so?"

"Not really, but I also don't think that even if he hit her she had the right to then go set his bed on fire while he was passed out in it."

"It didn't give her the right to kill him," I said. "Please remember, we are on the side of the law here. We're just trying to figure out what happened here, other than the obvious facts. We need to know everything we can find by the time this goes to trial."

"Fine," the blonde answered. "Horace probably wanted to go to bed with Lucy. She said no or resisted, so Horace may have slapped her. She looked around and found the kerosene and burnt him up. As far as we know, Horace didn't hit any other girls. For the most part, the girls liked him. Some felt sorry for him. He was a small, unattractive man who constantly drank too much. Those are all of the facts that we know. Why a jury would let a woman who murders a man by burning him to death, get off free, is beyond me, even if Horace hit her a few times."

•   •   •

I had never met Sister Theresa. My trips to the Holy Trinity Orphanage had been greatly reduced since Father Luigi's death; Sister Theresa had been put in charge of the girl's section within the past year. We met in her small office on the first floor. She was dressed in a full habit, but it didn't hide her young face, clear skin and bright shining eyes. I wasn't used to a beautiful nun, but here was one.

"Father Corcoran told me to expect you and to cooperate with you in any way that I could," she said. She had a very pleasant voice. "He also told me that you used to be a ward here."

"I was, Sister. Never adopted. I continued here until I could get into the police academy."

She gave me a faint smile. "I understand that you have become an accomplished detective."

I detected a hint of sarcasm. "I always try to do the best that I can."

"And now you are here to help with the disappearance of Rebecca Tilson."

"I will do what I can to help," I said. "So far, this is based on the request from Father Corcoran. What I mean is there is no evidence of a crime. I'm not sure I'm here as a police detective."

She paused for a moment to consider that. "Do you remember what it was like to be an orphan here?"

Now it was my turn to reflect. I was an unusual orphan. I knew who my father was and later learned who my mother was. I understood how I got placed in Holy Trinity and why I was never adopted. I was to be taken care of by the orphanage with financial help from my father, even though he never acknowledged it. I was to remain there until I became an adult or I left. "I remember quite vividly how life was here."

"Pleasant or unpleasant?"

"Mostly pleasant I would say. I had an excellent mentor."

"Father Luigi, yes. I have heard many stories from some of the older nuns. He was an excellent mentor but may not have been the most pious. I have heard that he drank like a sailor and that his talks were strewn with vulgar language."

Her pretty eyes had narrowed a bit. I smiled. "All true, but he took excellent care of me."

"Did you ever feel like getting out?"

I thought about that. I had it better than most, but the thought that I was no better off than in a prison ward crossed my mind many times. The thought of venturing out on my own had crossed my mind. In the end, I guess I'd been too afraid to try and leave. "I may have thought about it. I never took any action."

"And that brings us to Rebecca Tilson."

"You think she just ran away?" I said quickly.

She put up one finger to silence me. "Rebecca is a spirited one. Not a bad girl, but she is one with opinions. Very bright for a fifteen year old. I think she has a very good imagination. I think she could be adventuresome. She is also a very pretty girl and for her age, physically developed. She has the prettiest, curly blonde hair."

"Do you think that her imagination and love of adventure might have caused her to wander off on her own?"

"I have talked with the girls who shared bed space with her. None of them had any idea that Rebecca may have had about running away, but maybe she didn't trust them. I would encourage you to speak with her friends. They may be more forthcoming to you."

I nodded. "And what about the possibility that a crime has occurred and she was abducted?"

She nodded slowly. "As you know, we are strict here, but do not run the orphanage like a prison. Rebecca liked to take long walks, especially at night. She preferred it when she walked alone. The night that she disappeared she said she was going for a walk. She is usually gone for about an hour. When it got well past that amount of time everyone became quite worried and we informed Father Corcoran."

"Would it be possible to talk with her ward mates now. I have a little time."

"I have asked them to be prepared to talk with you. They are waiting in the library upstairs."

. . .

Compared to the meeting with the girls at Lustland, this was a total contrast. The three teen-aged girls in the library, dressed in their Holy Trinity garb, looked nervous and curious at the same time. They all stared silently at me as we entered the room. The three were sitting around a table. They were silent.

"Girls," Sister Theresa said, "this is Detective Moses. He is going to help us find Rebecca Tilson."

That little announcement caused little reaction from the three. One of the girls laughed.

"Is there something funny, Martha," Theresa asked?

The girl, Martha, blushed immediately. She was a plain looking girl, with a blemished complexion. "No, Sister."

This little confrontation caused a silence in the room. I decided to break it. "Are any of you aware of where Rebecca would go on her little walks?" I asked.

The three girls took turns looking at me, Sister Theresa, and themselves, but they said nothing.

"You are not going to get into any trouble if you know something like a secret," I said. "I am only here to help find out what happened to Rebecca. If you know something about her, it may help to find her."

One girl, very small and with freckles covering her face, raised her hand. "You have something to say, Susannah?" Theresa said.

Susannah blushed as well. She swallowed hard. "Rebecca met a boy on one of her walks. She told us his name was Robert. He works at that tavern down the street, The Crows Inn. He is an older boy and she told us that she likes him a bit."

The other two girls hung their heads, probably due to their breaking a vow they had made with Rebecca. "How old a boy?" I asked.

Susannah shrugged a bit. "Rebecca didn't know exactly, but she said she thought he was eighteen on nineteen."

When I left Holy Trinity I walked down to The Crows Inn, but they were not open for business yet. If Rebecca Tilson was smitten with this boy, Robert, he may have a good idea where she was. For now, I had to get back to the precinct.

.   .   .

George Loftus was sitting at his desk, smoking a cigarette and looking at the ceiling. I almost felt bad taking him out of his daze or dream, but I felt myself frustrated and needed someone to talk to. "Can't imagine that you are dreaming about one of our cases?" I said.

He exhaled a large plume of smoke in my direction and smiled. "I was, in fact, thinking of one of them."

I sat down next to his desk. "Care to indulge me in your thoughts?"

"I was thinking about this kid, James Jefferson," he said. "It seems obvious to me that James upset somebody. Maybe he was the greatest kid, trying to help his family and all of that, but maybe he was stealing some things. Maybe his people didn't know anything about it. Would you tell your family that you stole something? No. I think James might have been a thief and he got caught by the wrong people."

I shifted on the hard wooden chair. "That's your final thought on the matter?"

He took another drag on his smoke and exhaled above his head. "Look, I feel real bad for that kid, but I think he was in the wrong place at the wrong time. I don't think it was one person that strung him up. Whoever it was, they are not going to squeal on each other. Without any witnesses we'll probably never find out who did this. Those Micks are tight down there. Nobody is going to rat on anyone."

I heard what George said. I couldn't really disagree with him. I took a deep breath. "Have you given much thought to Lucy VonMara?"

He smiled. "Not a bad looking broad. I liked her."

"I didn't mean sexually."

"If this guy, Butross, slapped her around a little bit, like she said, maybe he deserved it."

"But torching him in his bed as he slept? Sounds a little crazy."

"I'll give her the benefit of the doubt. The guy sounds like he was a louse. She seemed pretty normal to me and he did beat her up."

Again, I couldn't really argue. I closed my eyes for a bit. That dull ache that had plagued me before pressed at my temples. It had been away when I was on leave.

"Did you find your missing orphan?" I had told George about Rebecca Tilson before I went off to Holy Trinity.

I opened my eyes up. "Apparently she goes for a of walks. This time she didn't come back. The girls that she rooms with said she may have gotten herself a boyfriend. I went by the tavern where he works, but they weren't open yet. I think he may know something."

Loftus stubbed out his smoke. "What if somebody grabbed her or convinced her to go with them? What if it's like that case you and Krause were on, where girls were abducted and forced into being courtesans?"

Gunter Krause, my former partner, and I had been asked to find the daughter of an Italian ambassador. This search led us to a group with no other than Christian Hanson, my nemesis, as its henchman. The group's purpose was to grab young girls, mostly immigrants, drug them and force them into being prostitutes. My temples tightened amid the remembrance. "I guess it's possible. The girl is attractive and shapely for her age."

George shrugged. "Girls of all shapes and sizes disappear in this damn city every day. She was in an orphanage. Maybe she just said fuck this and left?"

That seemed more likely, based upon what I had heard about Rebecca Tilson. "So you think we are wasting our time on James Jefferson?"

Again a shrug. "We ain't going to find who killed that black boy. As far as Lucy goes, I'd say she has a chance to go free."

I nodded but didn't really agree. In James Jefferson's case, there was always somebody who knew something. With Lucy, I didn't think we had the whole story. I was about to get up from the chair when a runner came up from the lower level and told us we had a visitor.

•   •   •

My first reaction was to tense up when I saw who our visitor was. I expected an attack from the lawyer Bradley Luke when I saw him standing in the meeting room. Like a few people, I was sure he had questions about what happened to Patricia Farmer. I was surprised when he smiled at us when we entered the room.

"Thanks for seeing me," he said. He looked paler than usual, like he never got out in the sun.

I felt myself relax a bit. "Is this a social visit, Mr. Luke?"

Again the little smile. "This is a meeting in the middle," he said.

"The middle of what?" Loftus asked.

"Our thought processes," Luke said. "I could have come down here earlier and questioned what you did with my former client, but what was the point. The girl was a menace to us all. Other than killing her, I would imagine she is in a place where she can't hurt anyone."

I wasn't going to respond, but I was curious. "So why represent people like that? You knew she was as responsible as anyone for the murders."

"Most of the times when I am hired to represent someone I have a pretty good feeling whether they are guilty or not. In most cases there is some level of guilt. With Patricia Farmer, I knew what that level was."

"You didn't answer my question."

"I represent them because I get paid to keep them from getting the worst possible sentence. In some cases I get paid quite a lot, like with the Farmers. You may find it reprehensible, but it is a living. I don't find it immoral. It is just something that I do and I do it well."

"And now you represent Lucy VonMara and I assume that is why you are here," I said.

"I understand that you paid Lucy a visit?" he asked.

"We had a nice little chat."

"I must ask why?"

"The two aldermen, who run this fine ward, are concerned that she may be able to slip the law and get away with murder. She told us a nice story that makes a little sense. She didn't deny torching Butross. Her claim of self-defense is going to be up to the jury."

He nodded quietly. "There is something about her, something that bothers me," Luke said.

"With this case?" Loftus asked.

"Not this one," he said quickly. "Lucy was beaten up by the man because she refused to do what he wanted. She retaliated. We'll see what happens there. It's just her. There is something about her, the way she talks, the way she describes things. There is a coldness there, a detachment. It's like she has no feeling for what she has done."

I laughed. "The son of a bitch blackened her eye and split her lip open. I can't say I blame her too much, right or wrong."

He face showed color for the first time, anger. "You don't understand, Moses. With Patricia Farmer, I got this same feeling. Even if she didn't physically kill those women, she enjoyed what was going on. She got a thrill out of it. I could tell by talking with her. It might not be the same with Lucy, but I can tell that killing Butross was no different than washing her laundry. It was just a mundane chore. Her manners chilled me."

"So what are suggesting?"

"I think there is something there, something in her past. I think she has an evil streak. I checked with my sources at the PD. There is no record of her committing a crime, but I feel she has and not a minor one."

I felt that familiar stab at my temples and saw a few flashing lights. I rubbed my eyes for a moment. This was something new. With Luke's description, I felt chills.

· · ·

I made the mistake of walking home that night. It had been a long day with no real clues, but a number of interesting thoughts on James Jefferson, Lucy VonMara and Rebecca Tilson. All of this jumbled information caused the tightness at my temples and the occasional flashing lights. It was a cool night; the moon was starting to shine and I thought the fresh air would do me good.

Whether it was intentional or not, I found that my path took me past Soon Lee's, the chop suey joint that doubled as an opium den. I walked past the place, deliberately not looking into the first floor dining area. I couldn't see the den; that was located in the basement. I hadn't gotten fifty yards past the place when I thought I could smell the dope and then I licked my lips. I closed my eyes and the taste hit me. The thought of that first drag off the pipe calmed me a bit, but I opened my eyes and there I was standing dumbly on the street. Anyone passing by would have thought that I was addled. I took a deep breath of the cool, night air and continued on.

It was still several blocks to my apartment. I knew Joan would wait for me, but she knew what my work was like. I was not a clerk. My hours took me all over and to many late nights. I didn't see anyone else as I walked along the Levee streets. I passed the poker rooms, bars, brothels and casinos. None of that interested me.

When I got up to Cooper's, I didn't keep going. I climbed the few stairs into the place. I had eaten dinner here many more times than I could count. I always sat at a table when I ate. Tonight I took a seat at the bar. I knew the bartender, Kenny, and he knew me.

"Haven't seen you in here for a while, Detective Moses," he said. He was a little man, probably weighed one-thirty soaking wet.

"I was on leave for a while, Kenny."

"I heard you was shot, saving some kid."

The scene flashed by my eyes. That night on the Clark Street pier, the bastard with the wig, getting shot in the shoulder, and then blowing out the wig wearer's brains. My temples tightened.

"You feeling okay, Detective?"

"Yes," I said. "Now I am."

"Something for you?"

"Sure," I said. "Whiskey. Make it a double."

Kenny quickly poured the drink and put it in front of me. I looked at it for a bit wondered if I was letting anyone down. Joan had helped me for months to stay clean. I felt that I would hurt her. I lifted the glass and could smell the whiskey. I put the glass to my lips and drank deeply.

I don't know what time I got to the apartment. I don't know how many drinks I had. I undressed myself quietly and got under the covers with Joan. I turned away from her. She either heard me or felt me enter the bed. She rolled towards me and put one arm around me. Her touch made me feel how much I loved her. It also let me know how much I had let her down. It was a while before I found sleep and it was not restful.

Chapter Three

This time the body was that of an older man. He was poorly dressed, really in rags, was skinny and had all gray hair. He was hanging from the roof line of an old shed in an alley behind 65th Street. There was no wind this morning so the body hung limply. He was staring straight ahead, eyes wide open, his tongue hanging out of the side of his mouth. The tongue looked like a snake.

"Wonder what this old son of a bitch stole," Loftus said.

"Think he was in the wrong place at the wrong time?"

"Not now, Moses," he said.

My head hurt quite a bit and I did realize that this was not one of the things I missed about the booze; the cool air helped me feel better.

There was a much smaller crowd this time, seven to ten people, all white, all Irish. Somebody had gotten to a call box and let us know about the hanging. Nobody seemed to know who the caller was. "Anybody see or hear anything?" I said. I knew the answer.

A red-haired man stepped forward. He was probably in his mid-fifties. I could see that he was missing a hand. "You know,

Captain," he said to me. He had a heavy accent. "These niggers would be a lot safer if they stayed on their side of the street. Sometimes I think they ask for trouble when they come over here."

I wasn't sure of his intentions with this little speech. "And why do you think that is?" I asked. "Do you know something about what happened here?"

A woman stepped forward. "Shut up, Thomas," she said to the man. She turned to face me. "He don't know anything."

"Do you?" I asked. She seemed in such a hurry to interrupt Thomas' comments.

"No, sir, but Thomas is right. Our people don't get along with them. Now this ain't right, but when they come over here they do ask for a bit of trouble."

The coroner's men had cut the dead man down and were preparing to put him in the cart for delivery to the morgue. Loftus walked up to me. He was holding a good sized length of rope. He showed it to me. It was medium gauge and new.

"Same type used to hang James Jefferson," he said.

"That could only mean one thing."

"Yeah," he said glumly. "Some bastard is hanging black people for the fun of it."

The bluntness of Loftus' remarks made my temples sting again. I watched as the coroner's men loaded the dead black man into the wagon. How many would we get I asked myself? If Loftus was right, there might not be a limit on the number of victims.

• • •

Big Jim Colosimo stared across his desk at me; his head was resting in his hands which had rings on all fingers. I had been welcomed into his office, but now he was looking at me like a teacher at a student who had done something wrong. Loftus was following up on an old case. I had gone to see Big Jim on my own.

"Can I offer you a whiskey, Detective Moses?" he said, sitting back. "It's Canadian and probably stolen."

I would have loved a drink or two, but after my late night visit to Cooper's I felt a little guilty. "No thanks," I said. "I can't be drinking what one day could become evidence."

He smiled. "It seems you have recovered from your injuries that you suffered on the Clark Street pier."

"I have. My shoulder is a little tender, but almost back to normal."

"I certainly am glad you didn't meet your demise on that pier. There are rats along there and, I'm not sure what they'd do to a dead body."

"I am grateful to have missed that."

"Yes, and now you have returned to try and maintain law and order in this lawless section of our fine city."

"God bless the Chicago Police Department."

He opened a decanter of whiskey and poured himself two fingers of it. He took a sip and seemed to be enjoying the taste. "You sure?" he said.

"I'm working, Mr. Colosimo."

He laughed. "You amuse me, Moses. I know of your past history, the booze and the opium. Addicted people can try and stay straight as long as they want but eventually they fail and they are right back on the bottle or sneaking into the basement den of Soon Lee's."

"I don't know what my future will bring, but for the time being, I'm trying to do my best to stay clean and sober."

He took another sip of his drink and placed the glass on his desk. "So you didn't come here to drink my whiskey and you came alone, no partner. Must be something you need?"

"I am looking for a girl."

"Most men are. What kind of girl do you want, white, black, Oriental?"

"It's not like that and maybe I wasn't accurate. I'm looking for information about a girl, a prostitute."

Jim spread his hands wide. "You think because I run several brothels that I know every whore in this city or even this ward?"

"I'm just asking. The girl I'm looking for information on is the one who burned up Horace Butross."

"Poor Horace," he said. "Always dipping into the help, so to speak, and this one girl apparently didn't want to play along."

"He did beat her up."

"This sets a very bad precedent for other brothel and casino owners. You upset the help and they set you on fire."

"The girl's name is Lucy VonMara. She hadn't been working at Lustland that long. I'm trying to see what her history was at other places in town."

"You think she had a violent past?" He seemed interested.

"Someone tipped us off that she might not be this little innocent whore who got beat up and took revenge in self-defense."

Again he spread his arms, the lights in the room twinkling off his rings. "Look Moses, I don't know every girl and I don't know that name, but I can ask. There are people that get me girls. I can ask and see what they know."

"That would be appreciated," I said. "None of these girls that you are offered are forced illegally into the trade?"

He tilted his head to the side. "Don't upset me, Moses. The places I run are clean and I've got clean women. There are plenty of women out there that I don't need to kidnap and drug them to get them to work in my places."

"But that practice is still going on?" I was thinking of Rebecca Tilson.

"I hear a lot of things, Moses. Some can help me and others can't. That trade, as vile as I find it, is still going on."

I smiled. "But I bet you have no idea who's involved in it."

"Not much, but I did hear that your best new friend, Rupert Finch, might be trying to break into the business. He's opened a joint on Wabash. He might be looking for cheap girls."

I nodded. "You'll let me know what you can find out about Lucy VonMara?"

"I always aim to help the police," he said. "Just remember when I might need your help."

•   •   •

We had sent an auto to get Sam Fuller to bring him over to the morgue on Federal Street. There was nothing significant about the old, black man who had been hanged. We just didn't know who he was. We were hoping that Sam would know him and maybe point us in some direction. I wasn't very confident.

The body was lying naked under a white sheet in a room in the back of the morgue. The light in the room was dim; the smell from the dead body was strong. Loftus and I placed a handkerchief over our noses; Sam Fuller didn't. He looked very nervous as I pulled the sheet back, revealing the victim's face. For a moment, Sam stared at the face and didn't react at all. Then he nodded and turned and walked from the room.

In the hallway, he was rubbing tears out of his eyes. "Man, that's old Oscar," he said.

"You knew him?" I asked.

"Everybody knew him. He just an old guy, made money sweeping floors and doing some dishes. Don't go telling me that he hurt someone or was stealing. He just an old man."

"What do you think he was doing over in Irish town?" Loftus said.

Sam turned angrily towards George. "He wouldn't go over there. He was old and poor, but he wasn't stupid. There's no way he went there on his own."

"What are you saying?" I asked.

"Somebody took Oscar over there. That's what I'm saying. Oscar's whole world was eight blocks square. He would never go over there. Somebody had to take him."

"Let me get this straight, Sam. You're saying that someone came into the black section and grabbed Oscar to take him over there to hang him?"

He looked at me, eyes wide. "That's it, Detective. This ain't about a boy or an old man stealing shit. This is about white folks killing black folks because they don't like the color of their skin. This is Klan shit."

My stomach tightened. I wasn't sure what to say.

"Let me tell you something else," he said. "You cops better figure this out. We ain't going to let them keep killing us without doing something about it. We're angry already. This keeps up and things are going to boil over. You mark my words."

• • •

Lieutenant Shipley was not in a good mood when we returned to the precinct. In fact he was livid. We were immediately summoned to his small office on the second floor and told to close the door. His anger showed in the redness of his face. "Another hanging?" he said.

"Yes," I said. "An older man this time."

"And what was he supposedly doing?"

"Nothing that we know of. Just a black man on the wrong side of the street," I said.

"Or one that was abducted from his side of the street," George said.

"Wait a minute," Shipley said. "You seem to think that this man was kidnapped and hanged. He wasn't stealing like the boy?"

I felt my own anger run up the back of my neck. "Who said James Jefferson was stealing?"

"That's what I heard, Moses."

"That might not be true. In fact, I don't believe he was. I think he was taken and hanged because he was black. Just like this old man, Oscar."

Shipley seemed to relax. His coloring returned a bit to normal; he sat back in his chair. "You don't think either one of them got caught stealing?"

George spoke up loudly. "I agree with Moses. The rope used to hang both of these guys was brand new, same gauge. I think it was purchased specifically to hang these two guys. I think the hangings were a signal."

"What kind of signal?"

"Our source, Sam Fuller, told us that things down there are about to boil over. Things are getting bad between the blacks and the Irish. I think these hangings are the beginning of some real unrest."

Shipley swallowed hard. "How do we stop this?"

George laughed. "We get the Irish leaders and the black leaders together for a little summit. Maybe then we can work out their little differences."

"I'm not in the mood for glibness," Shipley said. Color was returning to his face.

"We don't know, Lieutenant," I said. "We got called into a murder. Now we have a second murder. We haven't even begun to figure out who did this. How are we supposed to suppress a riot?"

Shipley sat back again. "I don't think that Central Station and City Hall are going to care for that answer."

Our little unit was started to investigate the more vicious crimes in the city. Most of these involved murder, trafficking or kidnapping. Civil unrest, riots, was never mentioned. There had been riots before, like the Haymarket thing in 1886, but I didn't think we we're equipped to handle any of that. I didn't feel Shipley's total frustration, but I was concerned. Something bad was happening on the southside. I thought George and I were suddenly in the middle of it.

· · ·

When I walked into The Crows Inn I could immediately smell the beer, whiskey and cigarettes. The smoke in the place gave it a foggy look. The place was crowded with people eating and drinking. I walked up to the busy bar and thought about ordering a drink but stopped. Self -control won that round. When the bartender got to me I flashed my badge and told him I was looking for Robert.

"What do you need with Robert?" he asked.

"I'm looking for a friend of mine. Robert might know something."

His look told me he didn't believe a word I said, but he told me to wait a minute while he went and found the boy. Those few minutes of waiting gave me the opportunity to realize how much I missed the little neighborhood taps. I was trying to stay sober, but it was tough.

The bartender returned moments later with a big, tough looking kid. Robert looked about eighteen or nineteen. He was tall and broad shouldered. His dark hair covered his ears and kept sliding over his eyes. He wore denim pants and had an apron covering his shirt.

"You wanted to see me?" he said. He looked right at me, challenging.

"Let's move over there," I said, pointing to an empty table in a corner.

We both sat down and he continued to stare. "I'm looking for a girl named Rebecca Tilson. She went missing from the Holy Trinity orphanage a couple of days ago," I said.

"I don't know anybody named Rebecca," he said a little too quickly.

"You sure about that? A couple of girls from Trinity said that Rebecca told them she'd met a boy named Robert who worked at The Crow's Inn. Anybody else named Robert work here?"

Before Robert could answer a bigger and older version of him came up behind him. This version was holding a wooden club and looked like he wanted to use it. "What the hell are you doing talking to my boy in my place?" the man said.

My first thought was that this was Robert's father; my second one was that I thought I might have to shoot him. I looked up into that angry face. "I am trying to find a missing girl. I heard that Robert may know something about her. I'm just here asking questions."

Suddenly the father cuffed young Robert in the back of the head; it wasn't a love tap. "This about that hussy from the orphanage I've seen you with?"

Robert flinched from the slap. "I've only talked to her a few times," the boy said.

"Tell this damn cop what you know so I can get him out of here. This doesn't look good for business," he said.

My tension eased; Robert rubbed the back of his head. "You only talked with her a few times?" I asked.

"Maybe three or four. I met her out in back. She said she liked taking walks at night. I thought she was pretty."

"You only talked to her?" I said.

"Something physical happen to this girl?" the father asked.

"Not that we know of. Right now she is just missing."

"I wouldn't harm any girl," Robert said. "Like I said, we talked a few times. I kissed her once or twice."

"Have any idea where she might be?"

"None," he said. "I haven't seen her in a few days."

"She ever say anything about running away from the orphanage?"

51

He thought for a moment. "I asked her what it was like. She told me it wasn't so bad. She said she knew she was probably too old to get adopted so she was just waiting until she could get out. She never said a word about leaving. I haven't seen her in a few days. I thought she liked me. I thought she would have come by to see me."

Now Robert seemed down that Rebecca might have left him behind. I believed the kid. He had seen her, but not for a while. He had no idea what had happened to her or where she might be.

"My boy doesn't lie, Detective," the father said.

I thought Robert's face told the whole story. "I believe him," I said.

• • •

Joan was awake when I returned to the apartment. I had been a good boy. I had nothing to drink and I was a little proud of myself. I ate the dinner she had prepared. There was little conversation. I sensed that something was wrong.

"Tough day in the store?" I asked.

"No tougher than usual," she said.

"Your feet okay?"

"My feet hurt every day, Patrick. I stand on them for nine hours."

I guess she told the detective on that one. I shut my mouth and helped clear the dishes.

We moved into the small living room. She was knitting something. I didn't know she could sew and found it amusing that an ex-prostitute had this talent, but based on how the evening had gone, I kept my mouth shut. I read what little news there was in the *Tribune*.

"I heard you come in last night," she said. She kept her head down on her project.

I looked up from the paper. "I'm sorry if I woke you."

"I could also smell you."

I felt like ducking behind the paper. I said nothing.

"I've been with a lot of men," she said. "I know the smell of alcohol. I smelled whiskey last night. Not just a hint, a strong smell."

I started to say something, but she cut me off. "I know it's hard, Patrick. I know it's not easy to just stop all that, but you were doing so well. I also know that the job you have, just dealing with the normal stuff in the Levee, could drive someone to drink."

Was it that, I thought? Was it the squeezing temples and flashing lights I saw? "I'm sorry," I said. "I was going by Cooper's and I thought I would stop and have a drink. I guess I went a little too far."

She looked up from the knitting. She wore a sad look. "I never asked before, but now I am. Please promise me that before you stop at any of those places that you will take a minute to think about what you are going to do. Promise me that you will at least give that a try."

I knew I had hurt her. I felt terrible. Her request was clear and it seemed simple. "I will promise you that."

She nodded slowly. "Don't think I don't know that there are enough things in your job that might kill you. You don't have to go doing the deed yourself."

When I thought for a moment about all of the bad people I encountered, the Hansons and people like Rupert Finch, I couldn't argue.

Chapter Four

The man's name was Matthew Bartholomew. He was very fat and he had a mustache that made me not trust him. He also wore a suit that looked like it would cost my annual salary. The cane he carried was topped off by a gold eagle on the top of it. With Bartholomew came a bespectacled man of about twenty-five and a very large, bald, black man who wore a black suit. They were seated in the meeting room on the first floor. Shipley, Loftus and I were on the opposite side of the table from them.

"Who did you say that you represent?" Shipley asked. His face was red again and his collar was pinching his poor throat.

Bartholomew cleared his throat. "I am the president of the Chicago Negro League. Mr. Brand to my left is my top associate. Mr. Jennings, with the glasses, is my secretary."

George made a sound that came out like a guffaw, but he quickly stopped that; I simply stared at the three of them. This was the lieutenant's show.

"And how may I help you?" Shipley asked.

"Well, "Bartholomew said. "You have heard from the mayor?"

"The mayor's office placed a call to me."

"Nothing was said about our mission?"

"I'm afraid not. I was told to meet with you and do what I could to help you."

Bartholmew laughed a bit. "It's important for you to know about our mission. We are here, in Chicago, to help with the struggling black community."

Shipley nodded. "And what kind of assistance do you think that the 22nd Precinct can give you?"

I noticed that Mr. Jennings, the secretary, was rapidly writing down every word that was spoken. His pencil seemed to fly across the paper.

"I'm sure you can imagine, Lieutenant, the terror that is going through that neighborhood at this moment. How could you not? Two innocent citizens hanged because of the color of their skin. The poor residents must be wondering how many more killings there will be. I can't imagine the fear they must be living with."

"Those are terrible events. I can imagine there is a bit of fear going through the community, but I'm not sure what you would like us to do."

Bartholomew's face went red. "I didn't think I'd have to spell it out for you, man. I want you to stop the killings."

Shipley's mouth seemed to drop open. For a moment, I wasn't sure I'd heard what Bartholomew said.

"How do you propose we do that?" Loftus said loudly. "You see, chum, we don't know who is killing these people. If we did we would have stopped the murders already. If you know who is hanging these people, please let us know. We would be glad to visit and apprehend them."

"Loftus, please," Shipley said.

"This is bullshit, Lieutenant. Stop the murders. What does this guy think we are trying to do?"

"I meant no disrespect, gentlemen," Bartholomew said. "I only meant that I hope this is one of your priorities."

"Murders are usually are top priority," I said.

Bartholomew pointed a fat finger in my direction. "When it's white people being murdered.'

This stopped us all for a moment. It seemed that the general populace had the feeling that if a black person was murdered the Chicago Police Department would just look the other way and hope the case went away.

"I can assure you, sir, that we look at each case, regardless of the victim's race, and treat them the same way," Shipley said.

Bartholomew smiled. "Then I will take your word that you will do your best to catch the person or people who are committing these evil acts."

• • • • •

I think we were all reeling a bit from the meeting with Bartholomew. It wasn't that often that private citizens walked into the precinct and critiqued our handling of a case. Shipley retreated upstairs to his office; George said he was going to get something to eat. I checked with Coogan at the front desk, but there were no messages for me from anyone. I hoped that maybe Jim Colosimo would find something out about Lucy, but I really hadn't given him enough time. Not sure what I was going to do, I turned from the desk and almost walked right into Sister Theresa. I know I shouldn't make these comments, but the outside cold air had added color to her cheeks and made her look prettier. The black habit got me to quickly get away from that thought.

"Detective Moses," she said. "I thought that was you. I didn't mean to sneak up on you."

"That's okay," I said. "You could have sent a messenger with a note. I would have come and seen you at the orphanage."

She took a step closer to me and spoke quietly. "There are certain things that are better spoken of away from Holy Trinity."

I took her by the arm and led her to the room we had just vacated. She took a seat in one of the chairs and immediately coughed. The room was saturated with smoke. "Would it be better if we talked outside?"

She waved a hand at me and laughed. "I'll be fine," she said. "I'm not used to this much smoke."

"Unfortunately, most of the people that use these rooms are smokers."

"I don't think God will punish them." The smile left her face.

"What can I help you with, Sister?"

"Two of the girls that we spoke with the other day came to see me. They asked me not to use their names, so I won't. They told me something interesting about Rebecca Tilson."

"I met with the boy she had met, Robert, down in his father's tavern. Said he had no idea where Rebecca was."

Her eyes sharpened. "You believed him?"

"I did. I saw no reason to not believe him."

"I don't mean to indict the boy. It's just that what I heard may point a finger at him."

I scratched at the stubble on my chin. "Why don't you tell me what you heard?"

"Both of the girls that I met with claimed that Rebecca was upset about something that someone had done to her. She told the two that she was ashamed of what had happened. It felt like a big sin to her. She was extremely worried about what might happen to her."

The look on my face must have told her that I wasn't following. "In the afterlife," she said.

"I see," I said. "So somebody did something to her that made her feel like she might get in trouble with God."

"That's it."

"And you think it might be Robert?"

"Not me. The two girls that I spoke with. Apparently, Rebecca had told them that she had seen Robert on multiple occasions. She told them that they had kissed. They got the impression that things may have gotten further than that, and that maybe Robert had forced some of this on her. This caused her to feel this remorse and that is why they think she may have run away."

I nodded. "Robert is the only name that ever came up?"

"Yes," she said, lowering her voice. "I have to tell you something else."

"Please do."

"We know about Robert a little. Rebecca is not the first girl to cross paths with him. He likes to flirt with our girls and he's a bit pushy. At one time, one of the priests spoke with his father but got brushed off. The whole family comes to Trinity for mass. The mother is a sweetheart. We've never involved her; we didn't want to hurt her, especially since nothing bad had happened."

"But now with Rebecca missing, you think that Robert deserves another look see."

Her pretty eyes seemed more alert. "That is what I am saying, Detective Moses."

· · ·

There are times when police work moves along at a brutally slow pace. This was one of those times. Loftus had gone to get something to eat and Shipley was brooding in his office. The meeting with Matthew Bartholomew had done nothing but raise our tension levels. The little talk I had with Sister Theresa raised new questions about Robert, but these were only suspicions. So far my meeting with Colosimo didn't produce any results, but I was hopeful he'd come up with something.

I sat at my desk, brooding myself, and thought to make notes on some paper. The cases were all different, but similarities existed. With the two hangings of two black men, I had to look at the victims. One was a fourteen year old boy who was a junk collector; the other victim an old man that made a little money sweeping out places. Zero connections there. The similarity was the rope used in the hangings. Almost brand new and of the same gauge. We had the same person or people doing the hangings, but why? Sam Fuller said there were rising tensions between the two sections of town. Was somebody trying to raise these tensions? I shook my head.

Lucy VonMara had been charged with murdering Horace Butross. There was no doubt that Lucy had killed Horace, but she claimed she did it after Horace beat her and she feared for her life. She had the black eye, busted lip and missing teeth to show that Horace hadn't treated her like a lady. I still wasn't sure this gave her license to kill the man. At first I was curious why Aldermen Coughlin and Kenna came to see us on Butross' behalf. Did they know that Horace could be a bit of a louse and were trying to cover it up? What was more unnerving was Bradley Luke's concern about Lucy. He had agreed to defend her for this case, but something in her demeanor had spooked him enough to come calling on us. This spooked me too and led me to call on Big Jim Colosimo.

My non-police work case, the missing Rebecca Tilson matter was intriguing, but I wasn't totally buying it. Despite Sister Theresa's assertion, I believed what Robert had told me. He may have met Rebecca a few times, may have gotten a little physical with her, but I don't think he knew where she ultimately had ended up. There was a lot of trafficking of young girls going on, this illegal abducting and turning young women into prostitutes. I still got the chills remembering what Gunter Krause and I had found years before, those sick and wasted girls in Blue Island. I wondered if Rebecca had fallen for an easy ruse to get her out of the orphanage but send her to a worse fate. I put that little thought aside. I would follow up one more time with Robert and ask him some tough questions. Hopefully, his menacing looking father wouldn't be there to impede me. I would also visit Rupert Flint and ask him about the girls he was recruiting for his new brothel.

I was making one more note on my paper when I saw George Loftus coming up the stairs. He saw me looking at him and stopped. He waved his arms, telling me to get off my butt and join him.

• • •

"There's been another murder," George said. "I just walked by Coogan and he let me know. We've got to get out there right away."

I thought of another body hanging from a tree. "A hanging?"

"No. This one was beaten to death. And, Moses, this one is a white man."

The scene of the crime was in an alley, behind a tavern, on 67th Street. The victim looked like an older man, but it was hard to tell. Somebody had bashed his face in and had left identification to the imagination. His clothes were old and tattered. Whoever he was he was not well off.

The crowd gathered near the body was all white. I didn't notice any blacks. I also didn't see the solemn silence I noticed with the two black hangings. The crowd was agitated. The two cops who were watching over the body had their clubs drawn, like they were expecting trouble.

"Anybody tell you who this guy was?" I said.

"One guy came up and looked at the body. He said, 'That's Whitey', and he walked off. I didn't hear anything else," one of the cops said to me.

"Why are they so riled up?" Loftus asked.

"They said the niggers did this," the cop said.

Whoever did it did a thorough job. When I knelt by the body I could see that where one sleeve had rolled up on his arm there were several bruises.

A man stepped forward out of the crowd, a tall guy, dressed like a common laborer. "What are you cops going to do about this?" he said loudly. There was a loud response from a number of the others gathered.

I got off my knee and approached the man. It was pretty damn cold out and this guy was not wearing a coat. He didn't look cold. "You know who this guy is?"

"You mean was?" the man asked.

"You know what I mean."

"His name was Whitey. He was just an old guy, never bothered anyone. Some people saw him near The Taproom earlier. He must have come out here and ran into the black bastards who killed him."

"You saw these black bastards?" I asked.

"Come on, Detective. You don't have to wear a badge to figure out who did this."

"So why'd they kill, Whitey?"

"Revenge for them two hangings. That's why."

"You seem to know a lot. Do you know much about the hangings?"

He smiled at me. "I know two of the niggers got hung. That's it. It's not a secret. I also know that Whitey was a revenge killing. Why else is he dead? Like I said, he never bothered anyone."

We left the two cops to watch the body until the coroner showed up. The crowd was angry, but that seemed to be as far as they wanted to go with cops standing around. If they were convinced that some blacks had killed Whitey, they were in the wrong place to try and enact revenge.

The Taproom was a small bar, maybe a dozen tables and a long bar that ran the length of the place. It was early in the day, and maybe the murder in back of the place had robbed it of patrons, but the joint was empty except for the bartender behind the bar. He was a man of normal height, well -groomed with dark hair and a neatly trimmed mustache. His white shirt had not yet been stained by the day's activities.

"I don't suppose you two would like something to start your day off," he said. "On the house, of course."

I wanted something, badly. "Thanks for the offer, but we'd better not," I said. "We are a little busy."

"I would guess a few murders in the neighborhood would cause that."

"It does take us from our leisure time," George said.

The bartender laughed. "How can I help the police today? My name is Danny Conlin. I own this fine establishment."

"One of your past clients appears to be the victim in back of your place," I said.

He nodded. "I heard it was Whitey. Not really a client. More like a vagrant. I would give him some food from time to time and a drink, but he never paid."

"So he was just a bum?" George asked.

"Maybe a little harsh, but yes. I don't think he was employed. I also don't think he was employable. You can see. He was always dirty and he never changed his clothes. I think he just lived on the street. I never let him in here. I always gave him his food out the back door."

"You see him last night?" I asked.

"I did not. If he was killed last night it was before he came to the back door."

"And you didn't hear or see anything out of line?"

"No, sir. Last night we were busy. The place was pretty loud. I could barely hear the orders I was taking."

"Let me switch topics for a moment," I said. "I'm sure you hear a lot of things. You hear much about the two black hangings?"

His eyes narrowed. "Unlike a lot of my friends and patrons, I don't hate the black people. I find what happened to those two to be disgusting."

"I appreciate your views, but I was more interested if you'd heard any rumors about who might be behind the killing?"

He shook his head. "I heard about the hangings, but that was in the papers. As far as who might be behind them, I have heard nothing."

"And you would tell us if you did hear something?"

"Most certainly," he said.

"Believe that guy?" George asked. We were making our way back to our auto. The coroner's van had just arrived.

"I do. Why?"

"He seemed a little too smooth and sure about his answers, like he thought about them before we got there."

"Or he was being truthful."

Loftus laughed. "Maybe he fooled me. We don't get a lot of honesty out here. Where to?"

"Let's go see Sam Fuller. He may know something about a vigilante movement."

•　•　•

We found Sam back at his little house. He didn't look very happy to see us. When we first met him I thought he would be an ally, helping us to figure out the hangings. Now I wasn't so sure.

"You're back here kind of soon," he said. He was standing in his front door; I didn't think he was going to let us in.

"There's been another murder," I said.

His look changed. "Another hanging?"

"Not this time. This time it was an old white man. Looks like somebody beat the hell out of him with a club."

He got a little smile on his face which made my gut tighten. "What did this old white man do?"

"I'm not sure he did anything. He was an old vagrant, a bum. He was beaten to death and left to die in an alley over in Irishtown."

"It's a tough city, Detective Moses. People get murdered all the time."

I laughed. "You don't have to educate me on that."

"Then why are you here?"

"You made some interesting comments about your people not sitting back and accepting these hangings."

"My people?"

"You know what I mean, Sam. What did you mean by that?"

He stepped outside and closed his door behind him. He suddenly looked larger. "You know exactly what I meant," he said, raising his voice. "An old black man and a black boy get hung for no reason, I doubt we're going to sit around and take it without acting out."

"Any idea who might have acted out in this instance?"

"No idea at all and I take it as an insult that you think I might have knowledge of who killed this old white man. How do you know that he didn't upset some of "his people" and they killed him? Why does it have to be a black man or men that beat him?"

I knew he was just saying that. "Right now, I don't know anything. I've got two black men and now an old white man murdered within a couple of miles of each other and I have no reason why any of this has happened. It sounds a lot like tempers are flaring down here. It sounds like there is a lot of hatred on both sides. I'm just trying to find something out so that the whole thing doesn't blow up."

"Detective, you are just one man. I don't think one man has the ability to stop the anger on both sides. It's been building for some time. I meant it when I said there was a revolt brewing. These murders are just the start. Things are going to get worse."

"These are just your thoughts?"

He smiled. "Just my thoughts."

• • •

"I'm not sure I believe that guy, Fuller," Loftus said on the ride back to the precinct.

"You don't?"

"Just a feeling. He's certainly upset about the hangings but showed no emotion or concern for the beating of the old white man."

"Well, let's see if he ever tells us anything that helps us with either set of cases."

We got back to the precinct and I saw Desk Sergeant Coogan wave me over. "A messenger dropped this off for you," he said. He handed me a sealed envelope.

"I'm going upstairs to fill Shipley in," Loftus said. "Then I've got to see a man about my Canadian booze case."

There had been a lot of stolen Canadian booze showing up in the district. Loftus had been trying for months to track it with no success. I waved to him as he went up the stairs.

The envelope was new and I had no doubt who it was from. I carefully tore it open and removed the sheet of paper inside:

"Maggie at Pleasure Corner" was all the note said. Big Jim Colosimo had provided the name of someone who knew a little about Lucy VonMara. I told Coogan I would be out for a bit; he seemed disinterested and I left the building. The Pleasure Corner was on the corner of State and 20th Street. I remember being in there once to quell a fight when I was on patrol, but that was years before.

The brothel was a two story job, like so many in the Levee. If you didn't know what trade was being plied there, you would think it was a large family home. I made my way into the lobby. It was mid-afternoon. The girls weren't performing yet; the place was quiet. I walked into a parlor and saw a black maid, dusting some of the counter space. She eyed me warily. "We ain't open yet, sir," she said.

I flashed my badge. "I'm not here to buy anything. I'm looking for Maggie."

Her look didn't change. Maybe she thought a white cop was only there to cause trouble and be of no help to anyone. "I can get Miss Maggie for you," she said. "You wait right here."

I didn't say anything as she went through a door on her left towards the back of the building. I sensed that Maggie was more than a courtesan. I looked around the parlor. The place was clean and neat.

The door opened again and a woman walked into the room. She was older, with gray hair and a neatly powdered face. She smiled and held out her hand. "I'm Maggie," she said.

I shook the hand. It was thinly boned and creased with veins. "I'm Detective Patrick Moses."

"Jim Colosimo's man said you might want to talk with me."

"Not you particularly, but anyone who might know something about a woman named Lucy VonMara."

"Ah, Lucy," she said. "What kind of trouble is Lucy in now?"

This peaked my interest. "Well, it seems that she started a fire which cooked her boss, Horace Butross."

"So that was Lucy?"

"It was in all the papers."

"I don't read the papers, Detective. They only tell you parts of any story and mostly they are not true."

I had that feeling about the papers myself. "Lucy has a habit of getting in trouble?"

"Lucy is a nice girl and she is very pretty. I liked her. Her problem is that she has an opinion on everything. She likes to argue. Sometimes I think she likes to argue just for the sake of it."

"Nothing wrong with that," I said.

"No, there's not. The trouble starts when you don't agree with Lucy. You see, she believes she is always right. Disagreeing with her sets her off."

"How so?"

"Now this is all conjecture on my part."

"I'm all ears," I said, smiling.

She didn't smile. "We were all at Heaven's Gate, maybe five, six years ago. I was a hostess. Lucy was one of the girls and very popular. There was another girl, Katie was her name. For some reason the two of them did not get along and I could never see a reason for it. They just didn't like each other and they would argue about anything. Several times they had to be separated before their disagreements became physical."

"That bad?"

"Anger, name calling and many accusations. The madam, Mrs. Kaiser, thought she would have to let one of them go to stop all of the fighting."

"But she didn't have to?"

"No. I'm afraid not. One morning, Katie didn't come down from her room. We went up and checked on her. She was naked in her bed, just lying on her back. Someone had cut her throat. The bed was soaked with blood. We called the police and they started looking for the last john who had been with her, but apparently they never had any luck tracking him down. It's not like we keep records. As far as I know, no one has ever been caught or charged with the murder."

"Where does Lucy fit into this little story?"

"Like I said, Detective, Lucy was very popular with the clients. She was doing very well. The arguing with people stopped. She was very pleasant. She could have made a nice living there, but then one day she was gone. No word to any of us. She just picked up and left. We heard she might be at several places, but she didn't keep up with anyone. She had no friends, I guess."

"But you think that Lucy had something to do with Katie's murder?"

"I don't think it. I know it. They were at the height of their little fights. Something was going to break and then one day Katie turns up dead."

"But no solid clues that Lucy was involved in the killing?"

"Just the fact that she hated Katie."

• • •

I wanted to talk to Robert again about what Sister Theresa had told me. What I didn't want to do was have another confrontation with his father. The man seemed to have contempt for the police. Getting towards winter in Chicago, it gets dark in the late afternoon. I knew there was an alley behind The Crows Inn; I also figured that Robert, with his dirty apron was some kind of kitchen help. I figured one of his tasks would be to take out the trash. I found a nice spot behind the place to wait and lit up a cigarette. Surveillance, not one of my strong suits, could be long and boring. I hoped my wait wouldn't be long.

I had been able to place a call to the Central Station about the prostitute named Katie who had her throat cut at Heaven's Gate. All of the records of the city's homicides were kept there. I told the clerk that the crime was five or six years old and that I was interested in talking with anyone who had investigated it. The clerk didn't sound encouraging but said she would try and find something for me.

Loftus was still out looking for leads on stolen Canadian booze so I'd been alone at my little desk, making notes and killing time before my visit to see Robert. I was surprised when Lieutenant Shipley came up and took the chair beside me.

"You look like you are contemplating something very serious, Moses," he said.

"Most of what we deal with is serious and unfortunately I find myself thinking about it a lot."

"I would imagine your thoughts have focused on what's happening over in Irishtown?"

"I have covered that topic."

"And?"

"Two blacks dead by hanging; one white man beaten to death with some sort of club. All pretty brutal."

He leaned back and rubbed his temples. "For some time people have been fearing that there could be real trouble in that area, racial issues."

"Our sole source thinks that things are escalating."

"Where do these murders fit in?"

"All three victims seem to be rather innocent targets, like somebody was trying to make a point by killing them. There is no other motive for the killings other than hatred."

"Do you think one side or the other is trying to incite something?"

"I thought that with the hangings. I think somebody struck back with beating the white man."

He nodded slowly. "The department authorized your little unit to look into unique crimes. This is one of them. Right now it looks like just murders, but I've got a bad feeling. I need you to find out anything deeper that you can. We can't have this situation blow up into a riot."

"As you can imagine, people we talk to on both sides know nothing."

"Moses, you are a good detective. Somebody knows something. Find it for me."

With that, Shipley got up and left me as quickly as he had arrived. Find him what, I thought? Two groups of people who didn't like each other. Now they had started killing each other. Would this lead to a larger riot? I didn't know and didn't have the first idea how to find out.

Shipley' challenge to me was still in my head when I heard a door to The Crow's Inn being opened and a man came through it carrying a large trash bag. It looked like Robert. I tossed my smoke aside and came up behind him. I took out a sap I was carrying and laid it across the back of his neck. "Don't do anything stupid or I will split your head open," I said.

"I hear you," he said.

"Turn around slowly and don't say anything until I say so."

The man turned around and it was Robert. The light in the alley was not great, but I could see the fear in his eyes. "I told you what I know when you came to see me," he said.

I swung the sap and got him on the knee. He fell to the ground, using some words I have never used. "I told you not to say anything."

He didn't answer but looked up at me as if expecting another love tap.

"Your daddy's not here now so I want some better answers."

"I don't understand."

"I hear that you've gotten physical with a few girls. Maybe these girls didn't want to get physical with you."

"I never hurt anyone."

"But you advanced yourself on some of them when maybe they didn't want you to?"

"Okay," he said. "A couple of those girls came around and they were getting all playful. I tried some things, maybe went a bit too far, and they complained. The nuns talked to my father. I stopped."

"What about Rebecca Tilson?"

Robert laughed. "Oh, Rebecca never complained. She came after me. I didn't resist or anything. She let me touch her."

He wasn't lying. "Do you know where she is?"

"I don't, Detective. There was nothing wrong between us. I saw her one day and then I heard she was gone. That's it. No talk or note between us."

"She ever say anything about running away from Holy Trinity?"

He thought for a moment. "I don't think so. I think she kind of liked it there. She was one of the older ones. I think she was kind of looked up to."

I had been one of the older ones, never adopted. I don't recall being looked up to. Sometimes I felt I was pitied. "Get up," I said. "Go back inside. Don't tell your father we spoke. If I hear that you did, I will come back here. Got that?"

"Yes, sir," he said.

"You hear anything about Rebecca you'd better get a hold of me at the 22nd."

He didn't say anything but scurried back to the rear door of the restaurant. I felt bad about popping the kid, but I needed to get his attention. I did but failed to learn anything. Robert and Rebecca had flirted. He said she was a little promiscuous. Could be. I saw no reason for him to lie to me about her whereabouts. She had either taken off or was taken.

• • •

I hadn't gotten home late and I had had nothing to drink, but I sensed a coolness in Joan's mood. I took into consideration that she had worked a full shift at Marshall Field's and then had come back to prepare dinner for us. Based on her former career, she was doing a very good job of becoming domesticated. She was working and keeping a home. I was just doing my job as a detective and not much more. Where I used to spend hours in places like Cooper's, I was now spending them in our little apartment. It seemed to be a tougher transition for me.

Dinner tonight was beef, potatoes and vegetables. I would like to say it was one of the best meals of my life, but that would be a lie. Most of it seemed kind of bland, but I kept my mouth shut and ate everything. Like I said, her mood didn't seem great. I didn't want to push it.

She seemed as disinterested in her meal as I was, moving the food around on her plate with her fork. She looked up at me. "What was you first wife like?" she asked.

The question brought an immediate tightening to my temples. What was my first wife like? "She was a very sweet girl, very caring, a great mother, too."

"How did you meet her?"

"Her family had been robbed. I was on patrol and went there on the call. I think I spent more time talking to her than I did looking into the robbery. We went for a walk the following evening; we were married five months later."

She smiled. "And your children?"

My children, a boy and a girl. I was working more as they got older. I'd have to say I barely knew them. I was trying to figure out who murdered a cheating faro player when my wife and children were killed during a fire at the Iroquois Theatre. My last view of my little family was at the morgue, fire burned.

"Are you okay, Patrick?" Joan asked.

"It seems like it was a long time ago," I said, "but it was only four years ago or so. It seems each day I forget more and more about them. I try sometimes, but I can't see their faces or hear their voices."

She reached across and touched my hand. "I didn't mean to dredge up bad memories."

I had seen so many bad things that my memory was clouded. I wasn't sure what affected me.

"Did your drug use start after your family died?" she asked.

I laughed. My drug use. I didn't drink or visit any dens while I was married or a parent. I was not an abuser before I was married, but not a teetotaler either. After the fire, I found comfort in whiskey, opium and prostitutes. "I would say the answer to that is yes."

She squeezed my hand. "Are you okay?"

Meaning the loss of my family or my hiatus from vices? I looked closely at her pretty face, the eyes sad at this time. "I find that I am still on the mend."

She nodded slowly and went back to pushing her food around on her plate. I finished my dinner and resolved to read the day's *Tribune* in silence.

Chapter Five

I didn't sleep well. Maybe it was the heart to heart with Joan. I felt edgy when I woke up and when I got to the precinct. I was early; Loftus was not. I wanted to talk to him about Lucy VonMara, but he didn't come in until nine-thirty. He didn't say anything to me when he arrived, sitting at his desk quietly arranging papers on his desk. I walked over and took the seat next to him. His eyes were bloodshot and I could see that he had not shaved. He smelled of booze.

"Tough night, George?" I said.

"Tough life, Moses," he said.

Not knowing what this meant, I went a little further. "You find your Canadian whiskey source?"

He laughed. "No, but I did find some whiskey, American I think. May have investigated it a little too much."

Telling him about Lucy wouldn't do too much good at this point.

"I also went by the office of that Bartholomew character, the one trying to save all the Negroes," he said.

"When you say, "went by" what do you mean?"

"Relax, Patrick. I just checked the place out. He's got a nice office on Wabash, under the El. Seems to have a couple of women working for him so maybe the place is legitimate."

The black population in Chicago had been rising so there was undoubtedly issues where they needed help. I just didn't think that Bartholomew butting his head into a murder investigation seemed right. That whole situation seemed to be a mess and I thought this was a guy who could make matters worse rather than better.

I was going to leave George alone when a runner came upstairs to tell us that we both had a visitor, a detective from a neighboring precinct. George looked aghast that he had to talk with someone.

"I can handle it," I said.

"No. I'll come along."

We went downstairs and met an older cop, poorly dressed and needing a haircut. He looked more like a tramp than anything. "You wanted to see us?" I asked.

His eyes widened, like he was shocked by the question. "You wanted to see me; I'm told. Name is Boggs, Harmon Boggs. I'm a detective with the 21st. I heard you wanted to talk about the whore, Katie was her name, the one that had her throat cut over at Heaven's Gate."

I turned towards George. "I did a follow up on Lucy when you were out based on a lead from Colosimo."

George just shrugged.

"You guys want to talk or what?" Boggs asked. "I'm a little busy."

We led him into a meeting room and closed the door. We all remained standing. I still couldn't get over how unkempt he looked. "You were the detective that worked that case?" I said.

He smiled. He had tobacco stained teeth, some which were cruelly crooked. "That surprise you?"

"Guess not," I said.

"I might not be assigned to a special unit like you two, but I'm a damn good cop."

George was standing next to Boggs. He rolled his eyes. "Get on with your story," he said.

"I'm just saying," he said, his eyes going from George to me. "I caught this case and went up to the whore's room. There was nothing surprising about what I saw. She was laying there with her throat cut, one little neat line, clean through. There was blood everywhere."

"Who originally found her?" I asked.

"A couple of the other girls checked on her when she never came back downstairs. The madam gave us a description of the last couple of johns this Katie had been with, but you guys know. Trying to find these fellows is a bit like the old needle in the haystack bit."

I couldn't argue with Boggs on that. Record keeping was not a great art in the brothels, casinos or opium dens. "Ever hear much about another girl, Lucy VonMara? We heard she had an ongoing rift with this girl Katie."

"Oh, that story? I heard about it and I tracked this Lucy down alter after the madam told me about this fight. Lucy went over to Madam Blossom's. I talked to her and she said they'd argued a few times, they just didn't like each other, but that was that. She had no idea who Katie was with that night and certainly had no idea who had killed her."

"And that was the end of the investigation?" I said.

He laughed again and spread his arms wide. "Fellas, this was just another dead whore. We get dead whores all the time down here. I couldn't spend that much time on it."

When I had thought that George was an unwilling participant, I was wrong. He smacked Boggs with a well-timed backhand and knocked the scruffy detective to the floor. Boggs, stunned by the cheap shot, began to reach into his coat for his revolver, but George was ahead of him and placed the barrel of his own against Boggs' forehead.

"Easy, George," I said. I was about ten feet away.

"What the fuck is wrong with you?" Boggs said, looking up at George from the floor. There was blood seeping from his newly split lip.

"These are people down here," George said. "I don't give a shit what they do for a living, they are people. The reasons you never made it past a grade one detective are treating them like they are less than that and the fact that you look like a bum. You might want to change your attitude."

"Holster your gun, George," I said.

George gave me a glazed look. For a minute, I got the impression that he wasn't even aware that he'd taken his gun out. He slowly took it away from Boggs' head and put it back in the holster.

"You two are crazy," Boggs said, standing. "I'd heard about you, Moses, but Loftus is crazier."

I had no intelligent response. "You're free to go, Detective," I said.

Boggs quickly left the room, closing the door as he left. I looked at George. He still didn't look right. "Maybe you need a little coffee and something to eat."

"Yeah," George said. "I think that might be a good idea."

•　•　•

We went to a little place that served breakfast. I had eggs with bacon and toast. George still didn't look well, but he did eat some toast and drank several cups of coffee. I asked him if something was bothering him.

"You know, Moses, you're a smart guy. I see you work this job every day. I see you deal with the dead bodies, the whores and all the other people who make this shithole tick, and I know how you feel. I can see where booze and opium can heal the soul, at least temporarily. It's just a faze for me. I'm fine."

I heard him and understood part of it but had my concerns. "Want to check out Madam Blossom's?" I said.

"Sure," he said. "I don't see Lucy as the murdering type, but I'll go along."

Madam Blossom's was on Dearborn, not far from the Everleigh Club. I hadn't been to see the Everleigh sisters in a while and thought that might be worth a shot. They knew everyone in the District. Maybe they could give me a line on Lucy.

Madam Blossoms was one of the nicer brothels. I'm sure Blossom tried to model her place after the Everleigh's, but she didn't have the space or the capital to make it that grand, but it was a nice place. We met Blossom in the scented parlor on the first floor.

"Lucy VonMara," she said. "How could I forget my time with Lucy VonMara?"

Blossom was maybe in her forties. She was still very pretty and had a shapely figure. I had heard she had been a high price courtesan who had saved her money to open her open place. "I'm thinking that maybe the time that you spent with Lucy wasn't all that great?" I said.

She laughed. "Don't get me wrong. Lucy was great for business. She is a real beauty and had a great sense of humor. The men adored her. She was a very popular draw here."

"Then what was the problem?" George asked.

"You don't look well, Detective," Blossom said to George.

"Do you have a medical degree?" he answered.

She turned to me. "Your partner is a little edgy."

"He needs a nap," I said. "What was the problem if she was so popular and good for business?"

"She couldn't keep her mouth shut. She had opinions about everything under the sun. Sometimes these opinions led to big arguments. Sometimes I think that she was stating an opinion just to start a fight."

This wasn't really news. Other people had stated the same thing about Lucy. "Who'd she argue with?"

"Anybody who disagreed with her or anyone who she disagreed with. Other girls, patrons or me. It didn't matter. It wasn't just arguments. She would get loud and sometimes obnoxious. It got exhausting."

"So what happened?" I said.

"It was really a tough decision, but I had to let her go. One of our better clients got into a fight with her and she ended up criticizing his looks, religion and manhood all in one sentence. He threatened to never come back and to convince his friends to do the same. He'd had a very big following. It would have hurt the business."

"But there was never any physical altercations?"

"No. It was just all of the little verbal stuff that never ended. When she got heated up in an argument she would get very insulting. Why would you ask if things got physical?"

"Maybe Detective Moses thought this poor insulted john might have ended up in a bad way?" George said.

"Not here," she said.

"What do you mean not here?" I asked.

"His name was Clinton Brooks. He had some sort of big job with the Stockyards. About a month after Lucy left here, Clinton Brooks was found stabbed to death in his apartment. He had a nice place on 31st, from what I was told. I was also told that the police have never solved the murder, didn't have one clue."

•   •   •

I decided to walk over and talk to the Everleigh sisters; George headed back to his apartment for a needed nap. The sisters knew everyone that was anyone in the city. They also knew more than anyone about the brothel business, the owners and the girls. Lucy VonMara seemed to have worked at the higher end places. She would be in the same class of houses as the Everleigh's. Maybe they could help me.

I found Ada and Minna in the dining room of their lavish brothel. It never ceased to amaze me about how everything shined and glistened in the place. It seemed new every time I was there. In the dining room, the two sisters sat at the large table with the usual spread of food before them. They both smiled when I entered the room.

"Detective Moses, we are so glad that you came to visit us this fine day," Ada said.

I took a seat between them at the table. A black maid poured me fresh coffee. The smells of the food on the table mesmerized me, but I wasn't hungry. "Can I ask why you are glad to see me?"

"We have had a theft?" Minna blurted.

Ada gave her a hard look. "Yes, that is the case. Someone stole a gold and jeweled cigar box from the sitting room. Very expensive. I'd say close to ten thousand."

I almost spit out my coffee but recovered. "Ten thousand dollars?"

"That's what I said," Ada answered.

"You have called the precinct?"

"Not yet, but it doesn't matter. You are here to answer our needs."

Our little unit was not set up to handle theft claims, but the one Ada described seemed significant enough to listen to. "Any idea who might have stolen the box?"

"Yes," Ada said. "We had twenty-eight guests last night. All visitors are kept on a list. Most houses don't keep these kinds of records, but we do. We know when the box was discovered missing. We know who had left the house by that time. We've got it down to about thirteen names."

I thought of my three cases and what I had done with them and how much more I needed to do. The sisters had helped me in the past. How could I say no to them? "Get me the list," I said.

Ada smiled. "But I doubt you came here about our missing cigar box?"

"I didn't. I'm looking for information about a courtesan that has worked in the district for several years."

"A missing girl?"

"No. One that has been charged with a murder."

Minna laughed. Ada smiled. "You're talking about Lucy VonMara. Sad about Horace Butros, but he was drunken pig from all accounts."

"You know Lucy?" I asked.

Ada nodded. "She came to see us a while back, looking for work. Beautiful girl and such a figure. It was hard not to take her in. It would have been such an attraction."

"Why didn't you take her in?"

"Believe it or not, Detective, we check out every girl that comes to work for us. As much as we wanted to hire Lucy what we heard back about her was not encouraging."

"Can I ask what you heard about Lucy?"

"Sure you can. We heard she was crazy."

I swallowed my sip of coffee kind of hard. It burned my throat.

"You seem surprised," Ada said.

"Not really. Not much surprises me anymore."

"This might. We had an interesting guest the other evening. He came in later than most guests, close to closing time. This one may surprise you."

I laughed. "Try and surprise me."

"A priest, one from your old home. Father Richard Corcoran. He comes in about twice a month. Of course, he is not wearing his priestly garb."

Now that did surprise me. I wasn't sure how to respond.

"The Catholics say a lot of things, but may not follow what they preach," Minna said and she laughed out loud at her joke.

I nodded. "That may be true."

Once I had the list from the sisters I said goodbye and headed into the precinct. Was this all true about Lucy VonMara? Crazy might be too light a term to describe her. Was she a murderess who had stayed under detection for this long? Everything, other than Horace Butross, pointed at speculation and opinion, but the information was piling up. I thought about talking to her directly about all of these accusations, but it seemed too early.

The information about Father Richard Corcoran made my temples ache. I wanted a whiskey badly but shook off that need. Priests couldn't marry. I guess that didn't mean they couldn't have normal desires, but those vows they took were pretty straight forward. It bothered me that Corcoran had strayed so far from chastity. Also bothered me that he had the money to visit a place like The Everleigh Club.

• • •

Freddy Miles ran a little pawn shop on Maxwell Street. He usually did a brisk business, moving legitimate items. What a lot of people didn't know was that Freddy was one of the biggest fences in the city. He made a lot more money fencing stolen items than he did from legal pawning.

"Oh shit," he said when he saw me come into his shop. Freddy was standing behind a counter which showed a number of items behind the glass; the shelves behind him were packed. "What did I do?"

Freddy was a sneaky looking little man with a short, dark mustache. "I don't think you did anything, Freddy."

"Moses, I thought you just worked murders. I don't know anything about any murders."

"Relax, Freddy. I'm trying to find something. If you picked it up, no problem. If you don't know anything about it, I will leave. But don't lie to me, Freddy. That would pose a great problem."

"I ain't going to lie to you, Moses. What are you looking for?"

"I'm sure you don't ask the people who bring things into you where they got them from?"

"We are a business that thrives on being discreet."

"Spare me the bullshit."

Freddy laughed. "What are you looking for?"

"Someone stole a gold and jeweled cigar box from the parlor at The Everleigh Club. This happened within the last couple of days. Like I said, you are not in any trouble."

Freddy shook his head. "I knew I shouldn't have gone in for that one."

"What one?"

"That damn box. Cost me five hundred. I knew the thing was worth a lot more than that. I knew I could make a killing on it."

"But?"

"But I knew the fucking thing had been stolen. I knew the cops would come prowling around. Sometimes I'm not the smartest guy."

"I'm not here to question your intelligence, Freddy. Do you have the box?"

Freddy bent down and opened an unseen drawer in the counter. When he got back up he placed a shining gold cigar box on top of the counter; the box had several diamonds affixed to it. Value might be one thing, but the box might only look good in a museum.

"You paid five hundred?" I asked.

"Cash. I'm sure you are going to ruin my day by telling me what the thing is really worth."

"Not trying to ruin your day, but Ada Everleigh says the box is worth around ten thousand."

"Shit."

"Which you are not going to receive."

"Think the Everleighs will give me a reward for returning it?"

"Doubt it since I had to come here to recover it."

"Then I'm out the five hundred."

"Unless you can remember who brought it into you and you tell me their name. Let's forget the part about the discretion."

"Jesus, I hate doing this, but since I'm a Jew I might not suffer."

"What the hell are you talking about, Freddy?"

We were the only two in the shop, but Freddy looked around like he was trying to make sure no one was listening. "There's a Catholic priest, he brings me stuff now and then. I think he works out at the orphanage."

"Father Richard Corcoran?"

He smiled at me. "You are a great detective, Moses, and I didn't have to give you his name. Maybe I won't go to hell."

"I'm pretty sure you're going to hell. How often does he bring you things?"

"That I really can't answer, but I'd say three or four times. Usually smaller items. I pay him cash every time. The stuff is never on consignment."

My stomach burned. "You knew the stuff was stolen?"

"Assumed as much, but the guy is a priest."

I felt my temples tighten and the lights flashed a bit. Father Corcoran likes to visit a whorehouse, financing the little visits by fencing stolen items. "Wrap the damn thing up in some wrapping paper. I'll go see the good priest and see how much money I can get back for you."

"You're a good man, Moses."

"Just wrap the fucking box, Freddy."

•   •   •

I left with the gold box wrapped in a plain brown paper. Finding a carriage over to Holy Trinity proved to be an issue. I had to wait almost fifteen minutes before I saw one and it had started to rain. When I got to the orphanage I was told that Father Richard Corcoran was in his office in the rectory behind the main building. Walking back there, I saw one of the girls I had talked to about the missing Rebecca Tilson. She waved at me.

"Can I help you find something, Detective Moses?" she said.

"No. I'm fine. Just on my way to see Father Corcoran."

This little comment caused a sour look. "I don't like him very much," she said.

She couldn't know about his thievery and trips to The Everleigh Club. "Why is that?"

She shrugged. "Nothing really. Just a feeling I get from him."

"I don't mean to press, but what kind of feeling?"

She thought for a moment. "I know he makes some girls uncomfortable. He gets a little close to them. I don't know. Just a feeling."

She walked away, but she had my attention. I went back to the rectory.

Father Corcoran greeted me in his first floor office. He looked tired. I wondered where he had been the night before. "I wasn't expecting you, Detective. Have you some news about Rebecca?"

"Nothing more than a boy at The Crow's Nest who seemed to have a little thing for her."

"That boy, Robert? He seems to like to pester some of our girls. We talked to his father but got nowhere. I assume he knew nothing?'

"Nothing of relevance."

He ran his hand through his hair. I placed the wrapped box on his desk. "A present?" he asked.

"Not really. This is a gold cigar box, stolen from The Everleigh Club, that I had to recover from a fence named Freddy Miles. Seems he paid the person who brought it to him five hundred dollars."

Corcoran shifted around on his chair. He went to say something but remained mute.

"I think it would be a good idea for the person who took this box to return it to The Everleigh Club. Then I think it would be a good idea if that person returned the five hundred dollars to Miles, before he thinks he got scammed and sent somebody to collect the cash."

Corcoran managed a weak, nervous smile. "I will see that the person who took the box returns it and I will also see that Miles gets his money back."

"As a cop, there are certain things that we do that can ruin us, make us lose our job. I'm sure there are several things that a priest can do that would cause him a great deal of trouble."

Corcoran's Adam's apple bobbed. "Well, of course."

"I would think that cavorting at a whorehouse, even one as classy as The Everliegh Club, would get a priest in a lot of trouble with the Diocese."

He went to speak, but I put up one finger to stop him. "I don't want to hear about any moment of weakness, or uncontrolled desires," I said. "I don't want to hear that you went down that road again looking for recreation."

He seemed to hear me. His look was somewhere between shame and fear. I got up and left, leaving Father Corcoran with his thoughts.

•   •   •

I needed a walk after my visit with Father Corcoran. The tightening at my temples increased and I saw the little, flashing lights. The cool air outside of the rectory brought some relief, but the whole conversation with the priest was upsetting, I understood the thing about desire. How could you control that? Resorting to frequenting a brothel didn't seem to be the answer. Stealing things to finance your brothel visits seemed non-priestly as well. It also bothered me what the friend of Rebecca Tilson told me about Corcoran. What else could this man be up to? He was one to watch.

I walked past The Crow's Nest. The place seemed quiet for this time of day. I wondered about Robert but didn't think he was a concern with respect to Rececca Tilson. He just seemed like a kid that got a little aggressive with the girls. I hope my talk with him straightened that out. As far as Rebecca went, I got the feeling that she may have gotten tired of the orphanage way of life and may have left. I considered this and then thought of someone abducting her and trying to turn her. A bad thought about Rupert Flint crossed my mind.

I went past the boarding house where Lucy VonMara was staying, but she wasn't home. I was glad about this. I didn't really know what to say to her. I didn't think that she would admit to the few murders that we'd heard about. I realized that talking to her would have been a waste of time. I did check with the landlord. She had no idea where Lucy was.

So, walking up the street towards the 22nd, it occurred to me that all we had on Lucy were some rumors that might be hard to prove. With the killings over near the black/Irish neighborhood border, we had nothing but dead bodies and a concern that a riot was brewing. How do you stop the flames of hatred? With my non-precinct case of the missing Rebecca Tilson, I had no idea.

The nagging headache continued. The thought of whiskey and opium nagged as well. The lure was almost too much, but I realized I had made it back to the 22nd. I walked up the stairs without the aid of either.

George Loftus was nowhere in sight, but I had a visitor who was sitting on a bench across from the sergeant's desk. Coogan pointed at him as soon as I entered the lobby area. Sam Fuller was sitting there, looking down at the floor, holding a watch cap in his hands.

He looked up as I approached him. He looked awful. "They took my Aunt Janine, Moses," Sam said. "They took her right off the street. She was walking from the store and they took her."

"Who took her, Sam?"

"Don't try and be smart with me," he said loudly, spit flying from his mouth. "Those white, Irish bastards took her."

Aunt Janine had gone to buy some groceries. The clerk at the store confirmed this. The bag of goods was found lying on the ground on the route that led her back to her home. There was no sign of the woman. There were also no leads as to who took her. No one saw or heard anything. With this lack of information there was no idea where to look. As darkness overtook the Levee, this mystery would remain until later. What I feared was the outcome. I knew I would need to be sharp tomorrow. I headed straight for my little apartment.

• • •

"How do you do it?" Joan asked.

We were sitting at our little table finishing our dinner. I had told her how my day went. There was no doubt that the conversation revealed I was letting my frustrations out. "How do I do what?"

"Your job," she said. "You just spent fifteen minutes telling me about murders, people stealing girls, and fights between the blacks and the Irish."

I shrugged. "I'm not on the detail assigned to get cats out of trees."

"I'm serious, Patrick. How do you make it through your day without going crazy? All you deal with is violent death, or other crimes that would make another person lose their mind."

How did I do it? It was clear from the tightening temples and the flashing lights that my mind wasn't equipped at all times to deal with what I saw. "I don't know if I can answer that," I said. "The Levee has a way of producing bad behavior. Sometimes it gets past the acceptable limit. It is my job to try and keep it under control."

"But still there is violence and murders; young girls continue to disappear right off the street."

"I can't and the department can't stop all of the crime. Why are you asking me this?"

It looked like she might cry. She wiped at her eyes with her hand. "It's just that I worry. I worry about the baby that we are going to have and I worry about you. It's been nagging at me since I learned I was pregnant. I have this fear that one day I will be a mother without a father to help me raise our child."

"I don't think that you have a lot to worry about. Police officers don't die that often in the line of duty."

"Maybe not normal police officers, but those that are around you seem to die at an uncommon rate," she said, raising her voice.

She was right. In the past two years I'd had two partners killed, one beaten to death, the other half of his head blown off. Was I the cause? Did I take unnecessary risks? "One of those men was killed because he went looking for some dangerous men on his own. The other was killed in a raid looking for a killer."

"And what about you? You were shot three months ago. If that bullet is three inches lower it destroys your heart. Don't you ever get the feeling that maybe your luck is running out, that you might be the next one killed."

My temples tightened. "I can't have those kind of thoughts and get my job done. Having doubts about what I'm doing can cause a great danger."

"But you're going to be a father. Doesn't that change things for you?"

I looked at her pretty face, tear streaked now. I had been a father before and had never thought of the dangers of the job while on the street. In the early days, I'd been stabbed and shot at. "I don't think it will."

She got up quickly from the table and ran into our little bedroom, the door closing behind her. I was left sitting alone with the dirty dishes and my thoughts. I had been as honest as I could be and I had hurt her. All I knew how to do was be a detective. What else could I do? I got up and begin to clear the table.

Chapter Six

The mystery of Aunt Janine was solved just after nine-o'clock the next morning. When I say solved, I mean we discovered where she was. Lieutenant Shipley received a note that there was a package for him that had been delivered at one of the rear entrances to the building. A young patrolman was sent to recover the package but ran all the way up to Shipley's office when he saw what it was.

Aunt Janine had an old rag stuck into her mouth. Her entire body had been wound in rope, same gauge as the hanging ropes. One loop of rope had been tied tightly around her thin neck. I'd say the rope killed her, but the temperature had dipped into the teens the night before so the cold may have gotten her. Her body had been dumped by a rarely used door. The killer hadn't been so brazen to leave her by the front door.

Shipley turned to George and me. "What's the message here?" he asked.

George looked better than the day before but went into a coughing fit before he could answer. "The message, Lieutenant?" I said.

"Why dump the body here, Moses? What are they trying to tell us?"

Clearly I had no answer. George stepped forward and knelt by the poor woman. I saw him reach down and pull a piece of paper out of one of her coat pockets that he could access. He opened the paper and read what it said. He turned to me. "It's for you," he said.

I took the paper from him; Shipley looked over my shoulder. In crude printing was the message:

Better figure a way to stop this, Detective Moses, before all of hell breaks loose.

"Suggestions, gentlemen?" Shipley said. We were back in his office; the door was closed. Loftus and I sat across the desk from him.

"It wouldn't be too hard to figure out that Moses is one of the detectives on the case," George said.

"That's not what I mean, George," Shipley snapped. "What do we do?"

George lit a cigarette and now, sitting closely to him, I could see that maybe he wasn't in as good of shape as I thought. I smelled booze again.

"Well," I said slowly, "it would help if we had a witness of any type in any of the killings. So far, nobody sees or hears anything. I get the feeling that if somebody is murdered on the other side, the other side cheers."

"What the hell do you mean, Moses?" Shipley was not in a great mood.

"I mean if a black person gets murdered, the Irish cheer or vice versa. These people are rooting for their sides. No one is going to turn in anybody."

"Jesus, this is going to blow up."

"It has blown up, Lieutenant. When word gets back to the black side of town what happened to Aunt Janine, I would expect that we'll see some sort of response. Probably not a good one."

"So, again, what do we do?"

"Can't police every street," Loftus said. "Can't bring everybody in for questioning."

"I think it's bigger than just one killer walking around doing this," I said. "This is some sort of organized effort."

"Like the Klan, "George said.

"God damn it," Shipley said quietly. "God damn it."

I knew George and I were dreading the drive out to see Sam Fuller to give him the news about Aunt Janine, but that venture would have to wait. The precinct received a call about the murder of a prostitute. Sadly, the murder of a prostitute wouldn't take priority in the Levee, but this one caught my attention. The woman had been killed in a brothel on State Street. The location was no more than three blocks from where Lucy VonMara lived. The prostitute 's throat had been cut.

•   •   •

There were a number of cops around the brothel on State. Murders sometimes gathered interesting crowds. On the walk over I'd had a small conversation with Loftus regarding what Joan had asked about the night before.

"So how do you do it?" George asked.

"I used to rely on booze and opium to forget a lot of things," I said.

"But you're being a good boy now."

"Trying to be."

"Well, that is the most fucked up idea that you have ever had. We deal with all of the filth of the world down here. Hookers, pimps, druggies, gamblers, people who steal girls, we have em all."

"So I should resort to the booze and drugs."

"It's working for me."

"Is it? You looked like hell yesterday and not a lot better today."

He stopped walking and stared at me for a minute. "Now you are a character judge?"

"Not at all. I'm just saying that maybe it is better on rough days to take a little time away from the booze."

Loftus just laughed at me, a real laugh. He started back down the street.

The brothel was called the Romantic Gardens. The place was an old, two-story frame building. I didn't see any gardens anywhere and the only romance you'd find there you would need to pay for. The girl had been killed on the second floor. Riley O'Donnell had been the first detective to respond; Harold Pinter had joined him at the scene. Both were standing outside of a room on the second floor.

"It's a God awful mess in there, Patrick," Riley said.

I had seen victims of Simon Kluge, slashed to pieces. I turned to face Harold. "Worse than Kluge?"

He nodded. "If not worse, the same."

The victim, a brunette, which was all we could tell, was lying on her bed, face-up. She was partially clad in bed clothes. The rest of the description was vague. Where we could see her neck, we could see that it had been cut clean through with an extremely sharp knife. Her face, what had been her face, had been slashed repeatedly, making her unrecognizable. The face, her clothes and the bed sheets were saturated with blood.

"Oh, my God," I said.

"Fuck," Loftus said. "You might want to rethink your current position on whiskey and opium."

I heard what he said but couldn't respond. My temples tightened and the flashing lights appeared on the sides of my head. I felt faint but gathered myself and took several deep breaths. "Let's find someone that knows something about this girl and who might have done this to her."

The madam was a husky looking woman with a few dark whiskers on her chin. She was sitting in a chair near the foyer with a glass of whiskey on the table beside her. Her face was ashen; she was staring straight ahead at nothing.

"You okay?" I asked dumbly.

Her gaze shifted to me, but her look told me nothing. "I'll never be okay. I've never seen anything like that and I never want to see anything like that again."

"You have a name?"

"Marion. Marion Crosby."

"And that girl upstairs, she have a name?"

"That's Alice. That was Alice."

"Any last name?"

"Mitchell. Alice Mitchell."

"Do you know the last person who saw Alice?"

She shook her head. "I wasn't here last night. Maybe Judith can tell you something, but she won't be here until later."

I nodded. "Anybody, any of the other girls, report any noises or commotion."

"I don't think so. I don't know. I went up to check on Alice because I hadn't heard anything from her. I wish I had never opened the door."

Until we could speak with the woman named Judith, there wasn't much more to discuss. If one of the other girls or a patron had heard something they probably would have reported it.

When we stepped out into the foyer, Harold Pinter was waiting for us. As usual, he looked tired and his glasses had slipped down on his nose. "Find anything useful, Harold?" I said.

"No murder weapon, if that's what you mean, but I can tell you it looks like a longer blade, very sharp and that the slashes were made by a right handed person."

"That narrows it down a few," Loftus said.

"If you catch anyone, Detective Loftus, "Harold said, "it could be important at the trial."

George smirked and lit a cigarette.

"There is a door that leads to the outside and some stairs," Harold continued. "It was unlocked when I checked it so I'm guessing anyone could have walked in there and found this girl if they knew where she was."

"Could have been anyone who randomly walked into the building and found Alice's room," George said.

"Just a random killer, picking a random girl in her room?" I said.

"We've seen crazier."

I didn't think so. "Let's go check on Lucy VonMara. I want to know where she was last night."

"Come on," George said. "That's too coincidental. Lucy is not responsible for every murder in the Levee."

"Humor me. She lives only two blocks from here."

The boarding house where Lucy was staying was right around the corner. Loftus complained about my hunch during the entire walk but stayed with me. The woman that ran the house seemed upset as soon as we mentioned Lucy's name.

"That bitch owes me twenty dollars," she said.

"I'm not here to help you collect it," I said.

"Aren't you the police?"

"We are."

"And you can't help me get my money?"

I smiled. "I can ask her about it when I talk with her."

"Good luck with that. I haven't seen her in a bit."

"Catch her when she comes home," George said.

"That's just it. She left and all of the things are out of her room. I don't think she's coming back."

Maybe letting Lucy out on bail hadn't been such a great idea. It appeared she may have skipped out.

"Can you help me get my money?" the woman asked again.

"If we can find her," I said.

"Well, don't go looking for a redhead. She died her hair completely black, dark black, like a witch."

My temples tightened even more. We thanked the woman, who didn't seem pleased that we didn't seem that serious about helping her with her monetary crisis and left the building.

"I thought Lucy was convinced she did no wrong," George said. "Looks like she might have left town. If she left, there's no way she killed Alice."

I wasn't convinced. "Let's find out what Bradley Luke knows. Maybe he was right. Maybe there is something off about that woman."

"Not now, though?"

"No. We'd better head back in and get out to see Sam Fuller about Aunt Janine. I don't think that meeting will be very positive either."

• • •

Word of the murder of Aunt Janine had travelled fast, too fast. Her body had barely been removed from the back of the precinct building, when there were visitors to see Lieutenant Shipley. Matthew Bartholomew and his two associates were sitting in the main conference room on the first floor; somehow they had notified Sam Fuller of the murder and he had joined them. Unfortunately, Loftus and I returned to the precinct at just the right time and were invited to the little meeting.

Bartholomew sat at the head of the long table. He was dressed in another expensive gray suit. Mr. Jennings, the man introduced as his secretary, sat to his left. His head was down. Sam Fuller, dressed in work clothes, was seated on his right. The man called Mr. Brand, a large, black, bald headed man stood behind Bartholomew. He was dressed in a black suit that didn't seem to fit him. His massive frame made the suit bulge everywhere.

Shipley was seated at the other end of the table. When George and I entered the room we were told to sit on either side of him. The whole set-up looked like an us versus them. I noticed the look on Sam Fuller's face. There was sadness there, but there was also rage.

"I demanded this meeting because of the horrific ending of the life of our dear Aunt Janine, a poor woman, seventy-two years old," Bartholomew said.

Shipley coughed and tugged at the knot of his tie. "She was your aunt, Mr. Bartholomew?"

For a moment the lieutenants sarcasm hung over the table. Bartholomew seemed to rise up in his seat, his face burned with color. "You know what I mean, Lieutenant Shipley. You also know that not treating this case with the seriousness that it deserves can get you in a lot of trouble."

"What makes you think that we are not treating the case seriously?"

Bartholomew let out a laugh, more of a grunt. "When we arrived here we were told that the two detectives investigating the case," he stopped to point at George and me, "were out investigating another case."

"That is true. There was another murder we had to look into. Unfortunately, the Levee has a way of getting people killed."

"Yes, it is a sad part of the city. Decadence is rampant down here," Bartholmew said. "What I don't understand is how the murder of a prostitute takes precedence over the murder of a kind sole like Aunt Janine? Does it have anything to do with the color of her skin?"

I have mentioned before that when Lieutenant Shipley becomes angry his face gets very red and gives the impression that his head might explode. I watched his face go through this transformation, but saw Shipley take three deep breaths. "That is an absurd allegation. We would never let someone's race or ethnicity determine what order we look into a case, particularly a murder."

"So what do you now plan to do with Aunt Janine's case?"

I cleared my throat. "When we spoke to Sam yesterday, there were no witnesses to Aunt Janine's disappearance. I would imagine that the same scenario is present today. When we speak to people in the area, no one seems to hear or see anything. It is rather frustrating."

"Perhaps you are not pushing hard enough," he said.

I let this comment pass. "I do have a question."

"By all means," Bartholomew said.

"There was a white man, simply known as Whitey, beaten to death behind a pub called The Taproom. I'm directing this to you, Mr. Bartholomew, but also to Sam Fuller. Do you have any idea who may have delivered the fatal blows to Whitey, just an old white man?"

Sam Fuller started to come out of his seat, but Bartholomew used a hand to grab his arm. "Are you insinuating that we know something about this murder, that somehow it was a retaliation for what happened in the black section?"

"The thought crossed my mind. We get the two hangings and Whitey, a harmless vagrant, gets beaten to a pulp."

"I find your comments reprehensible, Detective Moses. We are here to defend the rights of the negro in Chicago. Three people have been savagely murdered for no cause. We seek justice for those three. We have no knowledge who may have killed this man, Whitey, as sad as that is. What I will say is that the temperature in that part of the city is boiling. It is not a healthy environment."

There was silence in the room. Both sides stared at each other in a bit of a standoff. Again, Shipley cleared his throat. "We are doing our best, sir. We are not ashamed to say that we need help with these murders. You are working in that community. We need the community to help us. Someone must have seen or heard something."

Bartholomew shook his head. "The mayor is looking to reelection come the spring. He is strongly behind our push to make life better for the Negroes in the city. These cases, these lynchings, are exactly what he doesn't want to see. A lawless town is not good for reelection. With no movement towards solving the crimes in the next week, I will be forced to report to him that I think your Major Crimes Division, is a failure, from the top down to the detectives."

Shipley's Adam's apple bobbed against his knotted tie. "I appreciate the work that you do for the black community. We will do our best to close out these cases successfully."

Bartholomew knew the meeting was over. He stood slowly and his small following got up as well. They left the conference room with no further discussion. I wanted to talk with Sam Fuller, but he was out the door before I had a chance.

Loftus lit a cigarette and blew a large smoke ring into the air. "A change in the way we do things, Lieutenant?" he said.

Shipley gave him a dirty look. "Proceed as always, but please get me a goddamn suspect."

"On another note that might not make your day, Lucy VonMara has disappeared. Left her boarding house with no word of where she was going and an unpaid tab. We are going to track down Luke, her lawyer, to see what he knows," I said.

Shipley shook his head. "Find her Moses. Find her before the aldermen are back and they go complaining to the mayor as well."

. . .

Our first task was to see if we could find out anything about Aunt Janine and who killed her. We returned to the black section of town and I decided to avoid Sam Fuller. It seemed he had joined some union with Mathew Bartholomew. I wasn't sure what that was all about but didn't like where it was headed.

We walked the street where Janine was supposedly abducted but learned next to nothing. The people that she saw at the store where she bought her groceries, confirmed that. She made her purchase and left the store. Somewhere outside of the door, and within the short walk to her little house, she had been abducted. We knocked on every door of every house and business within that area. No one saw or heard anything. The time of day where she had been abducted was around dusk, not really dark.

"So someone just grabs this woman off the street and no one saw anything?" George said. He was standing on the corner, looking around. A cigarette dangled from his lips.

"Looks that way," I said.

"That's almost impossible. Two hangings and now a woman grabbed from the street in near daylight."

"Closer to night," I said.

"You could still see clearly. So, like I said, three people grabbed and murdered. Nobody sees anything."

"Gotta be extremely well planned."

He flicked away the cigarette. "What do you mean?'

"These weren't exactly random is what I mean. I think the victims were chosen based on who they were and what time of day it was, all grabbed when nobody else was around."

"But this is a busy street, at least busier than most."

That part bothered me. George was right. Three people taken and nobody hears or sees anything. It sounded impossible to me. "Somebody knows something."

•   •   •

"Where's Lucy?"

By the time we got to Bradley Luke's office it was late in the day. The lawyer looked as tired as we felt. There seemed to be a lack of energy, even in his face.

"I don't know," Luke said. "I haven't seen her."

"I think she skipped," I said. "We went by her boarding house and she was gone. The landlord said she had taken off and that she still owed twenty dollars."

Luke moved some papers on his desk. "She missed a hearing today. The judge was not happy and was generous enough to give me forty-eight hours to get her back in the courtroom before he sicks the bounty hunters on her."

"Was this judge the same one who gave her bail in the first place?"

"Long story."

"I don't give a shit how long it is; I want to hear it. We followed up on the little lead you gave us about Lucy and we learned a few interesting things. I'm thinking that she has a mean streak in her and it gets out of hand every once on a while."

Luke took a cigarette out of a pack, rolled it in his fingers, and then replaced it in the pack. "Judge Walworth awarded the bail to Lucy, but he is not the reason that she got out."

"Explain, please."

"It's quite simple, really. Lucy had a relationship with Judge Theodore, Austin Theodore. When she called me she told me to get a message to Judge Theodore. She told me to help her with a bail situation and she would be able to tell her truthful story."

"When you say relationship, can you clarify it for me?"

"Would you like me to paint picture for you, Moses? You are a smart detective. I'm sure you understand what I'm talking about."

"So what did you do?"

"I went and saw Theodore. I told him that Lucy was in trouble and she needed help from him in getting her judge to allow bail. At first he acted like he didn't know her, but then I mentioned to him that Lucy said she saw his wife and kids at the park on Sundays.

"This got his attention. He told me that he would talk to Judge Walworth and ask a favor if necessary. When we got to the courtroom, I wasn't sure what was going to happen, but after hearing Lucy's plea of not guilty, Walworth let her out on bail and at a very affordable sum."

"And you really don't have any idea where she is?"

"None. The hearing was at ten o'clock. She was a no show and now you tell me she's gone. Why are you so interested in finding her anyway?"

"I think she might have cut a prostitute's throat."

Luke swallowed hard. His already pale face paled even further.

"We don't know that for sure," George said, "but Detective Moses get his hunches?"

I looked at George. "No real hunch, but a real suspicion."

"Try Judge Theodore," Luke said. "He might have an idea where she went."

Outside, it was getting late and dark. "You seem to really feel that Lucy can do some bad things," George said.

"I do and I can see that you don't."

"I'm just willing to give her the benefit of the doubt. I don't think she's a bad person."

"Let's see what Judge Theodore has to say in the morning."

"Goodnight, Moses," George said and he turned and walked up the street.

"Goodnight, Loftus," I said, but George was far enough away that he didn't hear me.

• • •

"You seem like you are upset with me" Joan said.

"I'm not upset with you. I just need a little time to think about what I need to do next."

"I shouldn't have been so hard on you when I talked about your job."

"You weren't wrong. It is a dangerous job. There are a lot of potentially bad situations."

"That's what I worry about. You helped me get off the street. You are going to be the father of my child. I don't want anything bad to happen to you. I'm not sure what I would do if you weren't here."

These words, her expression of care for me, jolted me. "I will be careful out there. I will remember that there are others who I am responsible for." I said these words, but I knew it was not a good idea to be thinking of other things when people were trying to kill you.

"Any leads on who is killing the black people?"

"Not really, other than somebody who doesn't like them."

"Don't be smart. How about Lucy VonMara?"

"She went missing. There's something about her that strikes me in the heart. I think she is a dangerous person."

"But she's gone?"

"On the lamb. Nobody seems to know where."

"And I suppose you don't have much good news on your missing orphan girl?"

"No good news. No bad news."

"Maybe she just left the place."

"That's one theory. She wouldn't be the first, and Chicago is big enough to get lost in."

"Are you frustrated?"

Frustrated, I thought? What exactly was I? Three cases where we didn't know a whole lot, but each one was intriguing in its own right. "I wouldn't say frustrated. Lost and looking for answers would seem a better answer."

She got up and patted me on the shoulder as she headed for the bedroom. "You are a good detective, Patrick. I'm sure that you will figure out something shortly."

That was the second time that I had heard that about me today. My record indicated that I was a good detective. Today, I felt stupid. It was one of those situations where the only way we could figure something out was for something else to go wrong. One more bad thing could lead us out of the darkness.

My temples tightened and I saw the flashing lights. What I needed was some sleep. What I wanted was whiskey.

Chapter Seven

Judge Austin Theodore was an extremely fat man; for him it was a blessing that he got to wear the big robe. It hid his rolls of fat. Sitting behind his desk, wearing only his suit vest, you could clearly see where the fat strained the material. When we said we wanted to see him his clerk told us that he was unavailable. When we said it had to do with Lucy VonMara, we were let into his office right away.

"What has Lucy done?" the judge asked.

"As far as we know she has done nothing since she killed Horace Butross."

"And she has said nothing about me?"

I laughed. "She hasn't said a word to us about you."

He look relieved. "That's good. Why did you two want to see me about Lucy? I am a very busy man."

"We understand that, judge. The problem we are having is we can't find Lucy. It appears that she has left the boarding house where she was staying and she missed a hearing with the court."

"She's gone?"

"Looks that way. Do you have any idea where she might be?"

Now the judge looked a little nervous. "Why would you come in here and think that I might have an idea where Lucy VonMara is?"

"You helped arrange her bail."

"That is not true. Judge Walworth handled her hearing and awarded her to be released on bail."

"But you spoke to Judge Walworth and asked him to consider bail for Lucy as a favor to you."

Theodore's face got extremely red. "That is a preposterous statement, detective. I had no discussion with Judge Walworth."

"Okay, so when we talk with Judge Walworth, he is going to deny that you asked him for a favor for Lucy.?"

"Well, he should, because it isn't true."

"Not what we heard and it would probably not be good if Walworth contradicted what you said and something was made public and your family heard about it."

The judge sat up straight in his chair and was about to say something but stopped. He took a large breath. "What is it that you want, detective?"

"I want to know where Lucy is?"

"I don't know."

"Do you have any idea where she might be?"

"Can you tell me what she has done?"

"For sure, she has skipped bail, but that is not my concern. My concern is that I think Lucy is a dangerous person."

The judge laughed. "Lucy, dangerous? You can't be serious?"

"Detective Moses is not the joking type," Loftus said.

"What do you think, Detective Loftus?"

"I think Lucy is a beautiful woman who has suffered at the hands of a miserable bastard, but the bail jumping is not something to take lightly."

"I disagree with Detective Loftus," I said, "but we are not debating the issue. Who knows where Lucy is?"

The judge pointed a finger at me. "For obvious reasons, I do not want my name mixed up in this, but there is a man named Calvin Jessup. He does some private research and investigations for me. I told him to help out Lucy if she came to him. He may know where she is."

I relaxed. "How do we find Mr. Jessup?"

"Corner of State and 18th Street, three story brownstone, third floor. That's all I know."

"And if Lucy does get in touch with you, you'll be sure to tell us?"

"Anything to help the police, Detective Moses."

Outside of the courthouse, I turned to Loftus. "What makes you think our little Lucy is so pure and innocent."

"Don't be some damn judgmental, Moses. Nobody said anything about pure and innocent. I just don't think she's the murderer you make her out to be."

"It's just a hunch, George."

"I have hunches too, Patrick. Mine tells me she may have fucked up once or twice, but she is not a coldblooded killer."

• • •

George told me he had something to look into so I returned to the precinct on my own. We had to find the man Jessup, but I was more concerned with what was happening on the far southside of town. I wanted to speak with Sam Fuller privately. To see him join up with Matthew Bartholomew bothered me. Bartholomew seemed like a snake to me, but his society seemed real. He claimed to be here in order to help out the city's black population. Sam must have believed him. I wasn't so sure.

I needed to get a vehicle to go see Sam so I checked in with the garage and one was available. On my way downstairs I ran right into Sister Theresa. She was standing behind a line of people trying to voice their complaints to Desk Sergeant Coogan.

"Ah, Detective Moses," she said. "I was hoping to have a few words with you."

Again, I was caught off guard by her beauty, half hidden by the nun's habit. "I was just on my way to get an automobile to head to the southside. Let's step out in back."

We found a quiet spot near the place where Aunt Janine was found. I hadn't been thinking about that when I led her over there, but since it was cold it was a good place, out of the wind.

"How can I help you, sister?"

"I assume that you've had little luck in finding Rebecca Tilson?"

This was an understatement. The girl had left the orphanage and no one knew where she was headed. The boy, Robert, confirmed he'd had relations with her, but had no idea where she went or was. "Nothing, really."

"I told Father Corcoran that we should have made an official request of the police, not to keep it a private matter."

"It's one of those things that I can see either way. The whole department looking might help, but if you don't want the papers or Diocese to know about the disappearance, keeping it private seems logical."

"Rebecca was always a little rebellious so I suppose anything is possible with her."

"Any more ideas where you or any of the other girls about where she might have gone might help. Sometimes girls of that age protect secrets of their friends."

She smiled, the perfect teeth. "I was a girl once."

I considered this. What was her life like before she became a nun? "I just don't have much to go on and, admittedly, I'm stretched a little thin."

She nodded. "I think there has been a little bit of a development. I'm not that sure, but I do trust the source.

"But you are here to tell me?"

"Yes," she said. "I will not tell you the girl's name, but she came to me privately. She was in tears; she felt that she had sinned gravely."

"What was her sin?"

"Not her sin," Sister Theresa said. "It was Father Corcoran. The girl came to me and said that Father Corcoran had touched her improperly."

I felt the air come out of me. Father Corcoran, the thief and whorehouse visitor, now had a new allegation.

"I don't know how to approach him about what this girl has said," Sister said.

I took a deep breath to gather my bearings. "I will speak to Father Corcoran," I said. I felt my astonishment turning to anger. Who was this priest in real life?

• • •

Sam Fuller seemed reluctant to talk when I turned up at his little house. I looked for Loftus before I left the precinct, but he had not returned. Sam came outside and buttoned the coat he had worn. It was getting colder each day.

"I see that you have decided to join up with Mr. Bartholomew?" I said.

He looked up and down his street. Maybe he was nervous about who might see him talking to the police. "We have three people dead, three black people. These weren't bad people and they weren't committing any crime. And they weren't just killed. They were executed. We need a voice down here and I think Mr. Bartholmew can be that voice."

"I guess you weren't convinced that Detective Loftus and I would work the case as best that we could."

"Not really. What have you got so far, Detective? Like I said, three dead and no answers. We have more dead people than cops working the case."

I nodded. "That is true. We have talked to anyone that we can think of. No one hears or sees anything. People are snatched and hanged or hog tied right off the street. Seems impossible that nobody sees anything."

"What do you want me to say? That appears to be true."

"And this guy, Bartholomew, what does he say he is going to do for you?"

"You heard him. He's going to go all the way to the mayor and explain the problem. He is going to get the whole force involved if he has to. He promises to find out who's behind these murders."

"Let's forget the three murders on this side of the road. We have an old white man, not much more than a bum, beaten to death behind a pub over in Irishtown."

Sam gave me a wry smile. "Maybe he stole something."

"Don't think so," I said. "I saw it as a retaliation to the first two hangings."

"And Aunt Janine gets killed because of this old white bum?"

"Could be. Could be entering a vicious circle. It seems things are getting worse by the minute."

Sam turned his collar up against the wind. "What do you want from me, Detective?"

"Sam, I don't care what Bartholomew says or promises, I am still working this case. I'm trying to make sure that things don't completely blow up. What I want are witnesses. Somebody knows something, saw something or heard something."

"I understand that. What I want you to understand is that I know nothing. I know no one who knows anything about our dead people. I also know nothing about who beat up your old white guy."

"But you would tell me?"

He had to think for a minute before answering. This bothered me. "I would."

I thought for a second, making sure I didn't come off wrong. "Bartholomew pay you any money to help him."

"I'm upset that you asked that. What he said was that that he would bring aid to the community. I live down here. I can bring him knowledge so that he can present the needs to the proper people."

He wasn't lying about the money, but I still thought that he knew someone who had some knowledge of something pertaining to the murders. There was nothing new to learn so I returned to the precinct.

• • •

The big mystery when I returned to the precinct was the whereabouts of George Loftus. He said he had something to check after our meeting with Judge Theodore but had not returned since then.

"Where is Loftus?" Lieutenant Shipley said loudly when he saw me.

"I have no idea," I said. "I last saw him at the courthouse.

Shipley came up closely to me. "I've had some complaints about Loftus lately. I'm concerned about him."

I played dumb because that was the best I could do. "What kind of complaints?"

"Nothing terrible, but there's been some mention of the shape he's in when he shows up here. I've heard he's been hung over and smells of whiskey."

I had only seen George like this once or twice, but I had not been back that long from my injury. "I haven't noticed," I lied.

"And you really have no idea where he is?"

"None."

I saw Shipley bite his lip; I thought he might draw blood. "We've got to keep an eye on Loftus. It's something we don't need."

I didn't answer. I had my own history of being under the weather during work hours.

"This Bartholomew character is going to be a problem for us. He's legitimately set up to help the black community; the mayor loves the idea. He hopes he can bring some peace out there on the southside. I'm concerned he's going to bring us trouble."

"I'm sure he's asking for more cops to be put on the murders out there."

"That's why we'd better wrap things up out there and soon."

I took a deep breath. "We are trying to, Lieutenant."

"And find that damn Loftus."

I couldn't find half of the clues I was looking for and now I had to find Loftus. I wandered over where Riley O'Donnell was sitting. We hadn't spoken very much since our disagreement after the first hanging.

"Shipley didn't seem that happy to see you, Patrick."

"It's Loftus he's upset with. What's going on?"

"It's been that way for a while. George has been hitting the bottle a little hard. You know, chasing that damn Canadian whiskey has taken him into a lot of taverns and bars. Maybe he's gotten into tasting the samples a little too much."

I shook my head. "That's not it."

"What isn't?"

"George doesn't drink that much. For him to suddenly change that, there has to be something bothering him."

Riley shrugged. "Maybe he needs a mental doctor."

Maybe, I thought.

• • •

I had to carriage to the address where Bartholomew had set up his office for the Chicago Negro League. It was a long ride and the weather was getting colder as the afternoon wore on. As the sun ducked behind some of the buildings, darkness descended on the day.

The business with Loftus did nothing to soothe my aching temples; so far no flashing lights appeared. The situation with Father Corcoran clearly made my blood rise. In my time at Holy Trinity I had come into contact with a number of priests. The most damning thing I ever saw was one of them getting drunk and using foul language. What I had experienced with Corcoran was outlandish. I would visit him as soon as I finished with Bartholomew.

Without Loftus, I felt I needed to wait to see this man Jessup that Judge Theodore told us about. Loftus was my partner and in certain cases I felt it best if we did things together. Since he disagreed with me about Lucy, I decided it was best to hold off.

I didn't like the situation at all between the blacks and the Irish on the southside. So far four murders. No one sees or hears anything. It seemed unlikely. Why would anyone, like Sam Fuller, hold back anything if they knew something? I had no answer for that.

Like Loftus had said, Matthew Bartholomew looked to have set up a legitimate business. His office was located on the first floor and I could see that the electric lights were burning brightly and a number of people were busy working. I didn't get too close for fear of being seen so I couldn't make out who the people were. I did think what Bartholomew was doing was for a good cause. The blacks had been flooding into cities like Chicago from the south for some time. It was clear from what I saw that they needed some guidance. Maybe Bartholomew could help them. What I didn't like was his interference in murder investigations. Him riling up the mayor wasn't going to help us. Then again, if a riot broke out we would need all of the help we could get.

It was clear that I wasn't going to learn much more walking back and forth across the street so I decided now was as good a time as any to deal with Father Corcoran.

• • •

Father Corcoran was not at Holy Trinity when I arrived. I asked for him but was only told that he was out. Sister Theresa saw me for a few minutes, but she had no idea where the priest was. I wandered back outside and decided to walk. I went past The Crow's Nest. The place was crowded; I looked in the window and noticed Robert clearing some tables. Hopefully he'd learned his lesson about being aggressive with women. Time would tell.

I walked through the Levee as I had done before. I avoided the overtures from the streetwalkers who were out; I made sure to quickly walk past Soon Lee's. I didn't need an opium fix. What I wanted and decided to get was a whiskey. I stepped into Cooper's and took a spot at the bar.

"Detective Moses," Kenny the bartender said. "What are you having?"

"Double bourbon, neat," I said.

Cooper's had its regular crowd and they were out this evening. Had I wanted dinner I would have had to wait for a table. I wanted only my one little drink and then out the door.

Kenny placed the drink in front of me. "Kind of glad you stopped in tonight, Detective."

I sipped the bourbon, feeling its warmth hit my tongue. "Why is that, Kenny?"

"Your partner, Detective Loftus, has been in a few times."

I nodded. "He's been tracking a group that has been selling a lot of stolen Canadian whiskey."

Kenny laughed. "The only thing I saw him tracking was the three or four whiskeys that he had."

"That seems a lot for Loftus," I said.

"Sure it was, doubles, and it was just past noon. I asked him if everything was alright, but he brushed me off. Didn't seem like he was himself. I kept a close eye on him. He seemed to be mumbling to himself."

Some of this coincided with the irrational behavior that Shipley and Riley had mentioned. "Don't suppose you picked up on anything he was saying?"

"Can't say I did. As he drank more, he babbled more, but also became harder to understand."

I nodded but wondered. "Ever see me like that, Kenny?"

He laughed. "You were usually at your table, but any time I saw you at the bar, it was like you became more coherent as you drank, but you were mostly a quiet, peaceful drinker."

I couldn't tell if that was good or bad.

"Another guy was in here today asking if you still came in. I told him you did once in a while."

"Who was this guy?"

"He didn't say. He was very tall, big, long nose that looked like it had been broken a few times."

Kenny went to serve another customer. Loftus was here a few times, during the day, drinking a lot. Some big guy with a busted up nose was looking for me. Neither bit of news made me feel any better. I took one more sip of my drink, not finishing it, and left.

• • •

I went by Loftus' apartment building. I hadn't been there since the aftermath of the Simon Kluge case. I pounded on his door, but there was no answer. The landlord came upstairs to ask why I was making all the noise.

"Looking for George Loftus, the detective," I said.

"I know what he does, but I ain't happy with him."

"Why's that?"

"He hasn't been around much and he hasn't paid me for October and now it's November. When I do see him, he's been drinking and not friendly. I don't feel safe talking with him then."

"I understand. You ever see him with anyone?"

He smiled. "One time, not long ago, a couple of days. I saw him talking with a red headed woman in front of our place. I don't know if she'd been up to his place; he was trying to get her a carriage."

This talk might have explained his recent defense of Lucy VonMara. What wasn't explained was where George was and where Lucy was. My quick thinking detective instincts told me they were somewhere together.

"Can you tell Detective Loftus that I need my money when you see him?" the landlord said.

Now I was a collection agent for two landlords. I wished I'd finished my bourbon.

"Can you, Detective?" he said.

"When I find him I will tell him."

"It's ten dollars he owes. That's a lot of money."

I wondered quietly if he'd ever get his money.

• • •

I finally found myself headed for home. It had been a long day and nothing had been accomplished. Now, with these troubles with Loftus, I was even more confused. I had my head down as the wind blew around me; the cold of winter was not far off. I wanted my chair, some dinner and my paper. I smiled to myself. I was becoming domesticated. I heard a dog bark and I looked up.

It was dark and they looked like shadows, but there was a tall man with two large dogs about fifty yards in front of me. The man was very tall. I thought of what Kenny had told me about the man coming into Cooper's looking for me.

I took a few more steps forward, still unable to make out who the man in front of me was. The man and his dogs did not move. I unbuttoned my coat and my suit coat; the night wind chilled me. I took a few more steps. I heard the man utter a command and saw both dogs take off in a sprint towards me. It took very little thinking to realize they were not coming at me to get a pat on the head.

I quickly undone the snap on my holster and grabbed at the revolver. I got it out at the first dog started his leap at me. I fired and the Colt blew the dog out of the air; I barely heard it yelp.

I wasn't so lucky with the second dog. His leap caught me in the chest and knocked me down; the dog had to weigh a hundred pounds. The revolver went flying from my right hand. Even in the darkness, I could see the damn dog's snarling teeth with his open jaw. Reflectively, I put up my left arm as the beast went to bite.

He bit me on the arm, a bite that probably would have torn the arm apart if not for the heavy coat I wore. I felt the pressure of his teeth tearing at my arm. Holding the dog off, I reached for my right pant leg and the knife I always secured to my calf. The dog scratched at the side of my face. I closed my eyes as I felt a bone in my arm being crushed. I found the knife and pulled it from the scabbard. The dog's eyes were lit up to show the crazed frenzy he was under. I brought the knife up and stuck it in the top of the dog's head. There was no sound from it, nothing. His strength was gone and it simply slumped forward on top of me. My own pain had taken everything from me. I lay still on the pavement for over a minute. I heard the man who was with the dogs running away. My arm was throbbing. The scratches on my face were stinging and burning. The dead dog smelled. With the strength that I could muster I pushed the dog off me. I tried to sit up. I heard a noise behind me and instinctively turned, looking for my gun. It was an older woman, walking her own dog, a much smaller one than the ones who attacked me. Her little dog barked.

"Oh my goodness," the woman said, seeing the carnage in front of her. "Are you okay?"

There was no sense trying to play the tough guy. "No," I said. "I think my arm is broken."

She stepped forward and saw one dog with a good part of his head blown away and another with a six inch blade sticking in his.

"These dogs," she said. "Where did the come from?"

I finally got up from the ground. The arm was not good; I could feel blood streaming down my face. "Hell, I think."

· · ·

I made my way to my apartment and almost made Joan scream when she saw the looks of me. She cleaned up the deep scratches on my face; one of them wouldn't stop bleeding. We decided to get to Mercy.

The doctor that saw me, a younger one, was equally shocked by what he saw. "My god, what happened to you?"

"Got into a fight," I said.

"Patrick, the doctor is trying to help you," Joan said.

"Two big dogs attacked me."

The doctor still looked mystified, but first treated the bad cuts on my face and then looked at my arm. The arm was broken and would require being in a sling for a while. There was also several nice puncture wounds where the dog had bit through the skin. These were treated and bandaged as well. My face felt like it was on fire. My arm both ached and was aflame.

"I can give you something for the pain," the doctor said.

"That won't be necessary," Joan said. "Mr. Moses has dealt with pain before."

Back in the apartment, I ate my dinner and had a nice cup of coffee. I didn't feel very good so I moved to my chair. I didn't feel much like looking at the newspaper.

"So, tell me what happened," Joan said.

I knew I was in for it if I told the truth. One little lie wouldn't hurt. "I stopped by Cooper's looking for Loftus."

She crossed her arms. "Cooper's?"

"I behaved," I said. "Loftus has disappeared."

"Disappeared?"

"Maybe the wrong choice of words. He's been missing a lot of work lately. I hear he has been drinking a lot, sometimes while on duty. I went by Cooper's and Kenny, the bartender, told me George had been in there recently and had been drinking a lot."

"What does George have to do with the dogs?"

I laughed and my cheek hurt. "Nothing. I talked with Kenny about Loftus and he told me a very tall guy had been looking for me and asked if I went in there anymore. I didn't get a real good look at the guy with the dogs, he was some distance from me, but he appeared to be very tall."

"You're telling me that some really tall man let those dogs loose to attack you?"

"Well, that's the truth. The man was in front of me. I heard one of the dogs bark and he let them go."

"Jesus, Patrick. Who is this man?"

"I have no idea."

"This is what I'm talking about. You are going to be a father shortly and now you have a crazy man setting lunatic dogs loose on you. Those dogs could have killed you."

I was well aware of that. The dogs weren't trying to be friendly. "I don't know what you want me to say."

"I don't want you to say anything. I want you to think about your future, our future."

With that, she turned and retreated to our small bedroom, closing the door behind her. For me, unless I quit the force, my immediate future was suddenly looking for all sorts of missing people, a fifteen year old girl, a prostitute and my partner. I had no idea where any of them were.

My biggest case, the building fire on the southside, had me going nowhere. Now I had a crazy person trying to kill me with two large, unfriendly dogs. Who he was, and what his interest in any of this was, had me baffled.

Chapter Eight

This time the victim was a seven year old girl. She had gone missing from the back of her house around four-thirty the previous day. Some residents in a small house in Irishtown found her hanging from a small tree behind her house.

"Oh my, God," Riley O'Donnell said. He had been reassigned to me since George Loftus had failed to show up.

"You okay, Riley?"

"No, Patrick, I'm not. I was wrong. This is just some kid. What could this little girl have done?" Riley had four kids of his own; one I had saved from the Clark Street Pier less than four months ago.

The scene was more subdued than the last two, maybe twenty or thirty people standing around as the poor girl's body was lowered to the ground. Even with that number, there was little noise. This changed in a few minutes.

We were standing over the girl's body when there was a large commotion behind us. Riley and I turned to see a large group of blacks approaching the scene. It was a mixture of men and women. The black men were armed with clubs.

Most of the white Irish backed away from this angry group; they weren't saying much of anything. The blacks were hurling insults and getting closer. The four or five cops that were present stepped in between the two groups and drew their Billy clubs.

"Patrick?" Riley said.

I joined the small line of uniformed cops and stared into the crowd. It was a cold morning and I probably looked silly with my left arm in a sling and dog scratches on my face. I noticed Sam Fuller as the lead member of the black group. He took several steps forward; a cop stepped in his way.

"Let him go," I said.

Sam came up to me and tried to look past me at the body of the little girl. "Is it a little girl, Moses?"

"It is, Sam," I said.

He lowered his eyes and nodded. "Mary Jane Covington. Just seven. Now these son of a bitch Irish bastards are picking on little children."

"We don't know who did this," I said stupidly.

"Don't lump me into your category of dumb niggers," Sam said.

This time I nodded. "You should take your people and go back to your homes. Let us try and investigate this and figure out who is behind this."

"Four dead now, Moses. Four black people strung up like hogs. What have you proven so far, how evil white men can be?"

"Sam, you know we are trying."

"Mr. Bartholomew is right. Your small unit cannot solve this mess. It is too big for you to handle. I don't give a damn how qualified you are."

I wanted to respond, but what could I say that would make any sense. As I looked at Sam, a woman pushed past the line of cops and headed for us.

"Is that my Mary Jane?" she said. She was younger and pretty, but now her face showed anger and grief.

Before she could get past us to the body, Sam Fuller restrained her and held her back. "Don't go over there, LeeAnn," Sam said. "Let the police finish what they need to do."

"Why'd we come here?" she said out loud. "This is no different from Alabama. What has changed?"

I stepped closer to her. "Mam, my name is Detective Patrick Moses. I promise to do everything I can to find who did this to your daughter."

She looked me over and lunged forward; Sam held her tightly. She spit in my face. "All you white police, all you are is on their side. You can't do anything to help my Mary Jane. You can't do anything to help any of us."

I hung my head. Making false promises in this case was such an empty thing. "I am so sorry," I said.

She looked at me and the grief and sorrow etched on her face tore at my insides. "She was seven years old," she said. "Seven, Detective. She never hurt nobody and look what they did to her."

· · ·

If Riley hadn't been with me I'd have gone straight to Cooper's. As it was, we drove back to the precinct house in silence. When we got back we made straight for Shipley's office. We both had the same ideas on the situation on the southside.

"Good God, Moses," Shipley said. "What in God's name happened to you?"

"Two dogs tried to eat me," I said. "I look bad, but they are in worse shape."

"I'm really not in the mood for comedy, Moses. What happened?"

"Some very tall man let two dogs loose on me near my apartment. I shot one and had to fight the other one before I could stab it. Both of the demons are dead."

Shipley shook his head. "What very tall man?"

"I stopped by Coopers and was told a very tall man was looking for me. I guess he found me last night and decided that his dogs needed some exercise."

Shipley surveyed my injured face. "Is this attack related to one of our cases?"

I thought of the man Jessup that Judge Theodore told Lucy to go to for help. Could this man be the one who sicked the dogs on me and why? "I don't know for sure, but I intend on finding out."

"So what happened this morning?"

Riley grunted. "This time," I said, "our victim is a seven year old girl. I can't imagine that she was capable of upsetting anyone so much that they would hang her.

"Seven year's old. My God," Shipley said. "My own daughter is that age."

This was the first revelation that I ever got that Shipley had any life outside of the precinct building. I could see how the news affected him.

"What does this mean, Moses? Where is this all leading?"

I cleared my throat; I measured my words. "These murders are a sign. They are a sign of something evil brewing. It is white versus black. There is no other reason for it. These black people were killed because of the color of their skin. They probably did nothing wrong. The dead white man, he was a retaliation killing. He probably did nothing wrong either; he was probably in the wrong place at that time."

"And it will get worse?" Shipley asked.

"Based on this morning, yes. The temperatures on both sides of the street are getting hotter."

Shipley shook his head and changed courses. "Where is Loftus?"

"I don't know where he is. What I do know is that his landlord hasn't seen him in a while. He was last seen with an attractive redhead outside of his building."

"Who is the attractive redhead?"

"Not confirmed, but I think it is the murderer of Horace Butross, Lucy VonMara. She has also left the boarding house where she was staying. When last seen, she had died her hair a dark black."

"So Loftus has taken up with this VonMara woman?"

"It's just a guess, but yes."

"And they are both missing?"

"Yes. At this moment."

"Do you have any good news for me?"

Good news? "There's something about Lucy VonMara. There are stories about her temper and violent acts involving her. All talk right now, but I think the aldermen might be right. I don't think we are dealing with some sweet girl who killed Butross to protect herself. I think we are dealing with a killer."

"And Loftus is smitten with her?"

"She is very pretty, Lieutenant."

Shipley closed his eyes for a moment. "Find either Loftus or Lucy and you'll find the other. With the murders on the southside, what are we looking for?"

I laughed. "We are looking for anyone who has seen or heard anything that would tell us who killed these people. Right now, the answer to that is zero."

"Jesus," Shipley said. "Find someone, Moses. These killings can't go on. If they do we will have…"

"Chaos," I said.

He didn't respond to that. He just slowly nodded his head.

• • •

So I went looking for Calvin Jessup. Judge Theodore had told us that he advised Lucy to get ahold of Jessup if she had any problems. Since she had disappeared, I wondered if Jessup had any idea where she was. Maybe he also had an idea where George was, if Loftus had really taken up with her. It all seemed so preposterous, but it was all we had.

I got up to the apartment where Jessup resided and pounded on the door. I guess I was making a little too much noise because a neighbor came out of the door across the hall. He was a thin man, well dressed in a shirt and tie.

"You here about the dogs?" the man asked.

"What dogs?"

"That man, Jessup, the one who lives here, has two enormous dogs. They look like two rabid beasts. I have complained about them to the police, but they have never responded."

"These two dogs ever do anything to you?"

"To me, no, but they raise an awful ruckus when Jessup is not home. They bark and make all kinds of noise. Doesn't matter what time of day it is."

It was then, maybe as I stepped into the better light in the hall, that he noticed my scratched face and arm in a sling. "My God, man. What happened to you?"

"I am with the police," I said. "I doubt the dogs will be making much noise from now on."

"You have seized them?"

"Silenced would be a better word."

"Well," he said. "I suppose I should say thank you."

"I had no choice. Can you tell me what this man Jessup does for a living?"

He shook his head. "No idea. He works at different times. He's not a very friendly type."

"What does he look like?"

"He is very tall and very skinny. That much I can tell you. He has a very long and twisted nose. Looks like it was broken a few times."

"When was the last time you saw him?"

He seemed to consider this. "Couple of days. Maybe the day before last. He was leaving the building with his beasts."

So the man who let the dogs loose on me was Calvin Jessup. This was the same man that Judge Theodore told Lucy to contact if she needed anything. Apparently what she needed was to get me out of the way. Was it because we were finding out some very dangerous facts about her? What did she have going with Loftus? He knew what I knew about her. Was he protecting her? What was he getting back in return? Did Loftus know she'd had Jessup come after me? As I walked back down to the street level, my head was spinning. I had to come up with some of these answers and soon.

• • • •

I went looking for the lady named Judith who had been running Heaven's Gate when the prostitute, Alice, had been murdered. The woman I found was tiny, under five feet tall, and very slight. She looked more like a teacher than a madam. She looked tired and down.

"It's a terrible situation. I never would have imagined that something like that could ever happen. Alice was a sweet girl. It's just hard to believe that she's not with us any longer."

It looked to me like Judith was sad about Alice's death, but the brothel itself looked like it was getting ready for another regular evening worth of business. "I'm sorry as well," I said. "I'd like to ask you a couple of questions. If you're okay."

She blinked rapidly a few times. "Anything I can do to help the police."

I wanted to laugh at the usual comment but persisted. "Can you remember the last person that you saw Alice with that night?"

"That's too easy, Detective."

"How so?"

"I distinctly remember the man she was with. He was very tall and slender. He said his name was Jessie."

"He didn't say Jessup?"

"No he said his name was Jessie, clearly."

"Have you ever seen him before?"

"Never and I would have remembered. That was the first time I'd ever seen him."

"Did he ask to spend time with Alice?"

"Yes, he did." She grabbed my arm, the good one, rather hard. "Is he the killer?"

"Not sure. What can you tell me about the door that leads to the steps to the back of the building?"

She looked surprised. "That door is supposed to stay locked at all times. We tell the girls not to use it. We tell them if they get caught opening it, they will be fired."

If Jessup didn't do the murder himself did he open that door to allow someone else into the building. "How long have you been working here?"

She thought for a moment. "It will be eight years next month."

"Do you know a woman name Lucy VonMara?"

"Of course I know Lucy. She worked here for about a year and a half."

"And she knew Alice?"

"Yes. She knew Alice. Their suites were right next to each other."

"What kind of relationship did Lucy have with Alice?"

She laughed out loud and had to cover her mouth. "Relationship?" she said. "There was no relationship. If there was anything between them I would call them bitter enemies. I never saw two women like that; they couldn't get along. I'm surprised they didn't kill each other."

I wasn't surprised that maybe one of them had succeeded.

She must have seen the look on my face. "You don't think Lucy was involved? From what I heard, no woman could ever do anything like what had been done to Alice."

I thought about that comment before responding. Not knowing where Lucy, Jessup or George were I didn't want to tip anyone off. "I doubt that is the case," I said.

Chapter Nine

The following day Riley and I were summoned to a deserted lot near Chicago Avenue. Someone had found the body of a young woman who had been dumped in an area of large bushes. My thoughts went immediately to Rebecca Tilson, but I tried to remain positive that it might not be her.

The stand of bushes was circular, about fifty feet in diameter. In the middle of the bushes was a spot of open ground. Whoever had put the girl in there didn't take any precautions about hiding her. She was partially clad, but only from the waist up. She wore a torn blouse with a brassiere. Around her neck was a black scarf that had been knotted tightly. I assumed this was the instrument of death.

She wasn't very old; I'd say between fifteen and twenty. She was fully developed and may have been pretty except for the bruising on her face. She had a full head of bushy blonde curls. Since she wasn't wearing the Holy Trinity garb it was hard for me to confirm, but I thought we were looking at the body of Rebecca Tilson.

"From what I can see, she was strangled," Harold Pinter said. "There are a couple of defensive wounds on her hands which says she may have fought her attacker a little. The bruising about the face shows she was slapped or hit a few times."

"Any idea how long she has been here? I asked.

"The body has not decomposed very much and no animals have gotten to her yet so I am going to say maybe since last night, not much longer."

Riley was wiping at his eyes. When it came to the deaths of young people he took it very hard. "She's just a damn kid," he said. "Two in two days." He left the little enclosure.

"There's not much more I can do here, Patrick," Harold said. "We probably won't be able to learn much more until we get her to the morgue."

"There's a girl that has gone missing from Holy Trinity's orphanage. I think this might be her. I'm going to go pick up someone from there and bring her in for a positive identification."

Harold nodded and began the work of getting the girl out of the bushes. I went out to where Riley was standing, smoking a cigarette. "You okay, Riley?"

He looked at me and I could see the misty, red eyes. "This shit, this city, this district, it just takes it out of you. I don't know."

"Why don't you head in," I said. "I think this is a girl from Holy Trinity that was reported missing. I'm going there now."

"These are the bastards that if we catch them we should just shoot them. Why allow them a trial and any opportunity to tell their story. The hell with their story."

I didn't say anything. I patted Riley on the shoulder and went to find a carriage.

·　　·　　·

I didn't even think about the boy Robert when I got to Holy Trinity. The girl's body had been found several miles from the parish and an equal distance from The Crow's Nest. I wanted Sister Theresa to come with me to the morgue; I forgot about Father Corcoran even though I needed to speak with him.

"I'm surprised to see you this early in the morning, Detective Moses," she said. The look on her face showed concern.

"We have found a body. I'd like for you to come with me to make the identification."

"Is it Rebecca?"

"I'm afraid the description fits her. I need someone to verify it."

Her eyes dimmed. "Of course," she said.

We travelled to the morgue on Federal Street in silence. When death comes to someone it has a way of killing a little bit of those who survived. I could see that was happening with Sister Theresa. Her mind was totally on poor Rebecca.

Harold Pinter greeted us and led us to the lower level of the building. He led us into a large room that was filled with cloth covered gurneys, the unidentified dead of the last few days in Chicago. We walked a bit and stopped at a gurney. Harold offered Theresa a handkerchief. She looked bewildered but took the cloth.

Harold moved to the head of the gurney and pulled back the sheet that was covering the body. He stepped back and beckoned Theresa to step forward. She looked to me for a moment, but all I could do was nod. She stepped up close to the face of the body on the gurney.

She made a grunting kind of noise, like a sob, and put the handkerchief up to her mouth. She studied the face of the girl for a moment. She rubbed at her eyes and turned to me. "This is not Rebecca," she said.

My stomach dropped. "Are you sure, Sister?"

"Yes," she said. "Same looking blonde hair, but this is not her. I don't have any idea who this girl is, God rest her poor soul."

I stepped forward and pulled the sheet up over the girl's face. "I'm sorry, Sister. I thought for certain when I saw the blonde hair."

She grabbed my arm. "No need to apologize, Detective Moses. I can see some resemblance to Rebecca, but it's not her. I think you may have more than one girl missing in our little neighborhood. This seems to be a bigger problem for you."

Yes, it was. The girl on the gurney was not Rebecca Tilson. Who was she and more importantly, who had done this to her?"

•   •   •

The girl's name was Helen Gardner. Her parents came into the precinct shortly after my misadventure at the morgue. They reported that their daughter was missing. They had asked some of the neighbors and a few of her friends if anyone had seen Helen, but they had all said no. It appeared the girl had snuck out of her room on the first floor of their little home.

The parents had described Helen as fifteen years old, medium height with blonde, curly hair. This was a complete match with the girl we had seen in the morgue. I couldn't bring myself to tell them that their daughter was dead. They were both in such a state of dread that I felt I had to wait.

"She is our only child," the father said. "We tried to have others, but it never worked. She's a good girl, no trouble. We just don't understand." He was babbling a little, trying hard to hold back tears, but not succeeding.

"Do you get many cases like this where a girl just runs away?" the mother asked. "How often do they come back?" She said this through a full flowing of tears.

I could see that Riley was having a tough time dealing with this conversation. I was, too, but one of us had to take charge. "Do you have any idea where Helen may have gotten off to last night?" I asked.

They both looked at each other, looking for the right thing to say. "She was in the room where she slept around nine o'clock," her father said. "When she didn't come out for her breakfast this morning we saw that she was gone."

"I understand, but what about any idea where she had gone?"

"She's never done this," her mother blurted. "She's a good girl."

"I don't doubt that, Mrs. Gardner. I'm sure she is, but she went missing last night. I'm trying to find out what happened to her." As soon as I said it I resented those words.

"Do you think something has happened to her?" her father asked.

Riley looked at me and shook his head. "What I'm saying is we're trying to find out where she went."

Again the parents looked at each other. "We think she might have met a boy," the mother said. "I didn't tell Gerald because I didn't want him to be too harsh with Helen. I could tell by the way that she acted, like there were little stars in her eyes, that she had met someone. She never told me and I didn't ask, but I could tell. A mother can tell."

"She was too young for boys," Gerald said.

"No idea who this boy is or where she might have gone last night?" I asked.

"No," Gerald said. "We know none of that. That's why we came here. We need you to find our Helen."

I nodded slowly and took a deep breath. "This is hard," I said. Those three words and I saw them holding their breath. "We think Helen may have become a homicide victim. We have found a girl who fits her description. We'd like you to go down to the county morgue and make an identification. I know this is terrible news."

"A homicide?" the mother asked.

"You think our Helen has been murdered?" Gerald said.

134

"We believe so," I said.

This sent the two of them into a terrible fit of crying, a complete loss of control as their emotions flowed out. Riley said he would accompany them to the morgue. I don't think they heard him. I didn't think they heard or really understood anything at the moment.

．　　．　　．

I wondered about the connection between Helen Gardner and Rebecca Tilson. The locations where they had gone missing weren't that far apart. Helen had also reportedly met a boy; this story was similar to that of Rebecca's. Helen had ended up dead. Whoever had killed her hadn't taken that much time to hide the body. Rebecca was missing. I wasn't sure she was dead. I had no clear answer.

The situation on the southside was quiet if you call no murders in twenty-four hours quiet. Patrols had been dispatched in the area to watch out for any further developments towards an all-out riot. The patrols had also been asked to try and talk with anyone they could about news about any of the abducted and murdered people. So far, there was no news on that front.

My brain was telling me that Lucy VonMara was on a killing spree. Another dead prostitute, Alice Mitchell, a woman who had fought with Lucy, made this clear. The fact that she had gone on the lam solidified this idea for me. What baffled me was where George Loftus was. Had he taken up with her? What was wrong with him? The man called Calvin Jessup also seemed to be entranced by Lucy. Judge Theodore had given us his name as someone who was instructed to help Lucy out. Jessup was the last customer for Alice Mitchell the night she was murdered. Did Jessup carry out the deed for Lucy or did he let her in through the door on the second floor? All of these were questions that I wanted to ask Lucy, George or Jessup, but they were all in hiding. I was stumped.

I thought of what Sister Theresa had told me about Father Corcoran, the claim about him improperly touching a girl. This bothered me. Corcoran bothered me. I was asked to look for Rebecca Tilson. I had discovered that Corcoran had several flaws, but this wasn't really what I was supposed to be looking at. With respect to Rebecca, she was gone. Had something sinister happened to her or had she taken it upon herself to leave and do something else? My only thought on this was Rupert Flint. Jim Colosimo had told me that Flint might be recruiting young girls for his new brothel. I knew nothing about this, but maybe Flint could tell me something. Rebecca wouldn't have been the first girl to slide into prostitution.

• • •

It had been a while since we had talked with Rupert Finch. From what we had heard he had hired the two killers who went to rob Allen Price and his family. The robbery had gone bad and the entire family had been killed. It was also said that Finch sent the same two killers to kill Billy Baxter. We could never find any real proof that Finch was behind these murders, but we knew he was. When we tracked Arnold Perry and his still unknown friend to their little house near the Stock Yards, we could get very little information out of the two of them. The gunfight that ended up with both of them dead gave us little chance for a proper interview.

Finch's house on Michigan Avenue was as majestic as the lake that lay in the distance. He told us his business was finance. I didn't know what that meant, but I suspected wrongdoing. Whatever it was, he must have been good at it. The house was phenomenal.

When I went to ring the doorbell, I was fairly certain that Finch wouldn't see me, if he was even home. The door was answered by the same little Chinaman we had met before. "Is Mr. Finch at home?" I asked.

The Chinaman knew who I was. He eyed me warily. "I will see if Mr. Finch will see you, Detective Moses." He closed the door in my face.

I felt a little stupid standing there looking at the large oak door so I turned and faced the water. The day was starting to get old, the water looked to be a deep blue. Temporarily, I felt relaxed.

The door was opened moments later and the Chinaman, still looking miffed, held it open for me. "Mr. Finch says you get five minutes."

I had been in rich people's houses before. Thoughts of the Field's and Price's residences popped into my head. This one wasn't much different. Everything was polished and shined brightly. I was pretty sure that every item that I looked at I couldn't afford. Again, I wondered what Finch was up to.

Rupert Finch was not a big man, but he was tough looking. He seemed well tanned for this time of year. He was wearing a suit without the jacket, sitting behind a nice desk. He had dark eyes and a nearly bald head. A large scar ran across most of the top of it. He wasn't smiling.

"Come to accuse me of another crime, Moses?" he said.

There were two chairs in front of the desk. He hadn't asked me to take a seat so I stood between the two of them. "Not this time," I said.

"I am only talking to you because Jim Colosimo told me that you may be helpful to me at some time. Of course, he said there was always a quid pro quo involved."

I had heard Big Jim tell me how much he loathed Finch. Maybe there was a secret fraternity amongst the city's creeps. I let the comment pass. "Seems like an old line, but I am looking for a girl, a young girl."

Flint pointed at my face where the scratches were getting better. "Cat attack you?"

"More like dogs, two of them."

"And the arm?"

"They weren't as easy to kill as I thought they'd be," I said. "Like I said, I'm looking for a young girl who has gone missing. She was a ward at Holy Trinity Orphanage."

"What makes you think I know where this young girl is?"

"I heard you might be hiring some young girls for your new place."

He shook his head. "The women that come to work for me come voluntarily. Nothing insidious about that. I don't take on dopers, either. I'm trying to make the joint classy."

I nodded. "I don't suppose that you know a woman named Lucy VonMara?"

"Never heard of her. What did she do?"

"I think she's killing prostitutes."

He smiled. "Sounds like a charming gal."

"How about a tall thug named Calvin Jessup?"

"Moses, you know I don't go about hiring thugs. I am a legitimate businessman."

This almost made me chuckle, but I controlled myself.

"That's interesting what you said about the missing orphan girl. My manager, Teddy Kline, told me a Catholic priest had visited the casino. This, in itself, was kind of amazing. Teddy said he was shocked. Anyway, the priest wasn't interested in purchasing anything, but he was looking for a young girl, full figured, with blonde curls."

My gut tightened. Was Father Corcoran doing an independent investigation on his own. Was he going from brothel to brothel looking for Rebecca Tilson? Now I needed to talk with him right away.

"You see, Moses, I am not the grim criminal you thought I was. I am a smaller version of your friend, Colosimo. I wouldn't mind a little deal with you."

I wasn't sure what kind of deal he had in mind. "I'm listening."

"There are times when I hear things that are less than legal. I don't agree with some of these things like trapping women and forcing them to do things they don't want to do. When I do hear these things, I wouldn't be against tipping you off."

"In return for what?"

"Help, my friend. I don't know what kind at the moment, but we can play and trade if you want. Let's do it on an interim basis."

I was still thinking about Corcoran but heard him. In certain cases, good knowledge was hard to find. If he had some and was willing to share it, I might be able to help him some way."

"We can try it," I said.

"That's good, Moses. Sorry about your missing girl, but I have no idea where she might be."

I believed him. What I wanted to do with Father Corcoran was find out what he was doing in Flint's casino and ask him about what Sister Theresa had told me.

·   ·   ·

It was easier to get to Judge Austin Theodore's chambers than to find Corcoran at Holy Trinity. I walked up to his offices where a bespectacled clerk asked me who I was.

"Is the judge in?" I asked.

"I asked you who you were."

"I was here the other day. Is he in?"

"Let me see, but I can't see him if you don't give me your name."

I decided I was wasting my time and walked past his desk to the door that led to Theodore's chambers. There was a brief challenge from the clerk, but I was in the office before he could do much to stop me.

Theodore looked up at my entrance. He was looking at some papers and I startled him. "Moses, what are you doing here?"

I walked up close to his desk and leaned over it. I was tempted to grab him by his tie and drag his fat body across the desk. Good sense intervened. "Your friend, Jessup. Tell me about him."

"Like I told you before, he does some odd jobs for me. I asked him to look after Lucy if she needed anything."

"Does that include sicking two huge dogs on me?"

It was then that he noticed my scratched face. "My God. What happened to you?"

"Never mind. Where is Jessup?"

"I told you where he lives."

"He wasn't there. Tell me where I can find him and I don't have a lot of time."

"I don't know where he is."

"Does your wife need to get a visit from me?"

"What? Why would you do that to me?"

"Because the son of a bitch tried to kill me."

He looked frightened. I didn't know if it was the look on my face or the threat that I might talk to his wife. "I know he plays poker."

"Where?"

"The Midnight Lounge on State. He goes there quite a bit."

"I know the place," I said. "Just for your information, both Lucy and Jessup are missing. I went to both of their residences, but they are gone."

He shook his head. "Jessup is a bit of a simpleton. He's got a thing for Lucy. I think he fancies her. He does a lot for her."

"Would he do anything for her?"

The judge thought for a moment. "I think Jessup would do anything for Lucy."

"Including trying to kill me?"

"If Lucy told Jessup that you were bothering her in any way, I am convinced that he would come after you if she asked him to."

So there it was. Judge Theodore told Jessup to watch over Lucy, but he was probably doing that on his own. Now Jessup had tried to kill me. Lucy had probably told him to come after me. She must have an idea that I was on her trail.

.   .   .

"So you think that this woman, Lucy, hired a man to come after you?" Joan said.

"I think that might be the case."

"And he is the one whose dogs tried to tear you apart?"

"As far as I can tell. I haven't caught up to him, but the description I got matches the man who was with the dogs."

Joan shook her head. "And where is Loftus?"

"I don't know for sure, but I have heard that he might be cavorting with Lucy."

"This is insane, Patrick. The aldermen hired you to prove that this woman was not the angel she said she was?"

"As much as I dislike the aldermen, they may be right in this case."

She put her hands on her hips, standing before me as I tried to eat my dinner. "I'm not joking, Patrick."

I didn't remember telling a joke. "I wasn't joking about anything."

"This is exactly what I was talking about. You surround yourself with death. Eventually it will find you. In the four months that I've known you, you have been shot, mauled by dogs and had your arm broken. Does something really bad have to happen before you hear me? Will it be too late?"

I could see that she was on the verge of tears. "I don't understand what it is that you want me to do."

She wiped away one large tear. "I would like you to get out."

"Get out?"

"Quit, Patrick. I know that you have been hurt before, too, mentally and physically. I want you to get out before something awful happens to you. I want you to do it for me and the baby."

"But this is what I do. This is the only thing that I know how to do."

"You are an incredibly smart man, Patrick. You will find something else that you can do."

I laughed. "You mean like selling men's suits at Field's?"

"And what is wrong with that?"

"Nothing, but it's not for me."

"So there will be something else. Do you think the City of Chicago or the stinking Levee District would be there for you if something went wrong?"

I felt my temples tightening. The flashing lights in my eyes came next. "You don't understand. That's where we differ. I don't do it for the city or the Levee. I do it for the people who no longer have a voice. I do it for the ones who have been deprived of a full life. I'm the only one that they can count on for justice."

This made her think for a second. "I appreciate that. I really do, but who can I look to if you are not here? You did so well with the booze and the dope, but now I think you are sliding again. That and all of this death around you. I just worry that one day you won't be here and then what will I do? Where is the justice in that?"

I wanted to say something that made it seem like I was listening and cared. I didn't want to lie, but I'm not sure I succeeded. "Let me finish up these cases and then let me think about it."

I could see her relax a bit. "That's fair. Just don't let one of these cases get you."

Then I lied. "I don't think you need to worry about that."

She smiled and went into the kitchen area. I tried to eat but wasn't hungry any longer. My temples weren't as tight, but I was wound up. I was going out to look for Calvin Jessup. I thought I'd find him before he found me.

• • •

It was past nine-thirty when I got to the Midnight Lounge at State and 22ⁿᵈ Street. I had been by the place a number of times but had never been inside. The line on it was gambling, a small opium den and several unsavory girls. Jessup was a poker player. The card areas of these places were up in front so he wouldn't be hard to see if he was there. I had Riley meet me there but told him to take up a spot in the back of the joint if Jessup made a run for it.

The place was pretty crowded and overly smoky when I came through the front door. It wasn't well lit and it was hard to see. I moved deeper into the open gambling area. The tables were crowded and noisy. With all of the voices going at once, I couldn't make out much of what was being said.

It looked like they had three large poker tables and two for faro. All of the players were men. None looked like a tall person, but they were all seated. I got up close to the tables. Nobody stuck out. A dark haired woman approached me. She wasn't dressed in very much.

"Looking for someone," she said. Her toothy smile showed dark teeth and a big gap up in front.

"I'm looking for a friend of mine. I was told to meet him here."

She looked a little disappointed. "This friend have a name?"

"Sure. Jessup. Calvin Jessup."

She shook her head. "Sorry. Don't know him." She walked away from me.

I worked my way a little further into the room near the back of the place. I didn't see anyone playing poker that I thought might be Jessup. I saw a door in the rear that would lead outside. I figured I'd go tell Riley the night was a waste.

Just before I was able to get to the door, I was grabbed from behind by two arms that felt like a gorilla. I was crushed against this man's chest and forced through the door. Outside, another man reached into my coat and grabbed my gun. He threw it to the side; I was tossed onto the ground.

"I'm a police officer," I said.

"That right?" the gorilla said. I couldn't make out the face, but he was short and wide, very thick.

The second man, same size, but a skinny guy, came up close. He was holding a wooden club. "We heard you were looking for Calvin."

"That's right. Calvin Jessup," I said.

The skinny guy got closer. The club was in a position to be swung. "Calvin told us some men might come looking for him, wanting to kill him."

"Not me," I said. "I just want to talk with him. My badge is my wallet."

"Could be a fake badge, Sammy," the gorilla said.

From out of the shadows, I saw Riley emerge. He had a shotgun levelled at the back of the head of the gorilla. Neither goon heard him come up. He put the barrel of the gun up against the head of the gorilla. "That's enough, boys," Riley said. "That is a Chicago Detective on the ground and I am one as well. I have both barrels cocked and from this range both of your heads are coming off."

Sammy, the club bearer, dropped it onto the pavement. The gorilla seemed to shrink in size.

"Get up, Patrick," Riley said.

I picked myself off of the ground and proceeded to kick the gorilla very hard in the balls. He took my place on the ground. Riley held the shotgun at Sammy's head. I went to get my gun. I came back with it and placed the barrel inside of Sammy's left nostril. "You know where this fucking Jessup is?" I asked.

"No, sir," Sammy said. Up close he was a young looking punk. "He just told us to help him out if anyone came calling for him. He gave Luca and me a hundred. We didn't know you were the cops."

"Did you think I was lying?" I said.

He laughed. "Everybody lies in the Levee."

I couldn't argue with him on that. I took the gun away from his nose. "When did he tell you that?"

He shrugged. "Day or two ago."

"You're not bullshitting about not knowing where he is?"

"I have no idea where he is or where he goes after he leaves here. That's the honest truth."

I swung hard with the pistol and hit him on top of the head. He went down hard, but he was not out. I knelt by him. The gorilla had stopped groaning. "The next time someone tells you that they are with the police, try and believe them first. The other thing, this Jessup, if he comes in here, you tell him Moses is after him."

Riley and I walked out of the back of the alley, leaving the two thugs on the ground. I think they got the message. Riley was breathing hard. I asked if he was okay. He said his heart was hammering away. He had never shot anyone. I asked him for one more favor.

We climbed the stairs to the apartment that Jessup had rented. I had my revolver in my good hand; Riley had the shotgun ready. I told him we had to be quick. I raised my right leg and slammed it into the door. The door flew open easily. Inside the place, ready to kill, we found nothing. The bed in the center of the room was empty. We looked around. There was no sign of Jessup. There were two bowls lying on the floor to be used to feed dogs. They wouldn't be needed any longer.

Before we parted for the night, Riley stopped in the back of the precinct. "It was a terrible thing taking those Gardner parents to the morgue to see their daughter. The poor mother wouldn't stop crying; the father looked like he was in complete shock."

I had seen my own children and my wife in the same morgue after the fire at the Iroquois Theatre. I didn't remember how I felt at the time. I felt a burning in my throat hearing what Riley was saying. "I don't suppose you heard anything that might help us find the killer?"

"The father, the only time he mentioned anything, was mumbling about some boy that Helen had met. When I asked him who this boy was he told me he didn't know. He thought Helen she was too young to be having a boyfriend. He didn't think the Mrs. knew who the boy was either. I couldn't get a word out of her."

The night was getting very cold; a light snow had started to fall. Winter was approaching. "The orphan that's gone missing from Holy Trinity, she told her friends that she had met a boy, same kind of story. This girl, Rebecca Tilson, was a spitting image of Helen Gardner, shapely with blonde, curly hair."

"But you don't have any reason to believe that something bad has happened to Rebecca Tilson?"

"No body found, yet. The fact that Helen wasn't found that far from Trinity and the same story about the boyfriend bothers me."

"You think we have someone preying on younger, blonde girls?"

"It's not a lot, but it's something."

"I'm headed out early tomorrow to talk with some of Helen's girlfriends. Maybe they'll know something."

"There's a priest at Holy Trinity who's been acting awfully peculiar. He's the one that originally asked me to look into Rebecca."

Even in the dark, I could see Riley's eyes widen. He was a devout Catholic. "Patrick, you don't think that a priest could be behind any of this?"

I didn't want to argue this late at night, but a priest that ventured to whore houses, stole expensive items, and investigated the girl's disappearance had my attention. "I learned a long time ago, Riley, that it's best not to exclude anyone from an investigation until you were one hundred percent sure they weren't involved."

"It's not a priest," Riley said. He turned and started up the stairs to the building. The discussion was over, but I wasn't convinced of anything.

Chapter Ten

The morning was cold and bright. The nighttime snow had left a layering of two inches on the ground. My walk to Holy Trinity included many instances of slipping and sliding. My shoes were in bad shape when I got to the orphanage.

Father Corcoran was in his small office on the first floor when I got there. He didn't look very surprised to see me. "Detective Moses, you are out awfully early on this cold morning."

The warmth of his office made me shiver. "I wanted to speak with you before I had to head into the precinct."

"Please have a seat," he said. He wasn't acting like someone knew his secrets or anyone that had done anything wrong.

"I don't suppose that you have heard anything new about Rebecca Tilson?" he asked.

"I haven't heard much of anything," I said.

"I'm afraid that Rebecca may have tired of her life here and has run away. She's a smart girl. I am assuming that she has run far enough away that we won't find her."

This remark caught me totally off guard. "So what are you saying?"

He let out a deep breath. "Rebecca would not be the first child, male or female, who has run away from an orphanage. I'm saying that I think we shouldn't spend more time looking for her. I think she is gone."

The look on his face bothered me. "You would like me to stop looking for Rebecca, but you went to Elegance looking for her on your own?"

The look didn't change. "I had heard through an acquaintance that that establishment was taking in younger girls and putting them to work. I thought that they might have seen Rebecca."

"And what harm is there to keep on looking for her?"

He shifted on his chair. "None, I suppose, but I am not confident that you will find anything. We will not be filing an official police report. I don't see the point."

"I will probably keep looking."

He smiled. I didn't like him one bit. "I can't stop you."

"There's a couple of things that I think you should know."

For the first time he looked a bit uncomfortable. "What would that be?"

"One of the female wards here has complained that you might have touched her improperly; you made her uncomfortable."

The only tell was the deep swallowing movement of his Adams apple. "That is untrue. I try to restrict my physical contacts with all of the female wards."

I nodded. "Okay," I said. "The other thing I wanted to tell you was that there was a murder of a young girl, fifteen, not far from here. The girl bore a striking resemblance to Rebecca Tilson, a blonde with a full figure."

"That is a sad story."

"Yes, it is. Because of this news, I am thinking that poor Rebecca may have met a similar fate."

He laughed. "This is a vicious city, Moses. I am sorry about this girl, but just because she looked like Rebecca, a blonde with curly hair, doesn't mean there is a connection. I don't want to sound glib about Rebecca, but I just think that she ran away from this life."

He was stubborn but wasn't totally unbelievable. "I really don't believe that you should remain a priest."

This brought a different look to his face. "I don't believe that is up to you or any of your business."

"May not be, but if I hear that you are anywhere near any of the brothels in this city I will make a personal visit to the diocese and report you. If I hear that you have stolen anything, I will report you. One more time I hear about you getting close to a girl in your ward, I will report you. Are we clear?"

He didn't look very upset. "I have made mistakes. I have sinned. I have asked God for his forgiveness. My conscience is clear. I realize that I am only human and we all err at times. We have flaws. I am committed to being a better person and to serve this church and orphanage."

The little speech sounded rehearsed. I stood and buttoned my coat. My shoes hadn't dried very much. "I have made many mistakes in my life," I said. "I am trying to be better, as well, but I am aware that I may slip again. I know how that is, but I am not a priest. I will be watching, Father Corcoran."

• • •

I was not surprised that Lieutenant Shipley wanted to see Riley and I when I got into the building. He didn't look happy and his tie was knotted tightly at his neck; his face a bright red. "Any news of Loftus?"

Riley grunted. "His landlord has not seen him in a while," I said. "Other than he was spotted with a red-headed woman who may have been Lucy VonMara."

Shipley shook his head. "Do you really believe he is running around with her?"

"I'm not sure," I said. "I believe he may have become smitten."

Shipley shook his head. "So is she an angel or the devil?"

"Closer to the devil, I would say. There are a number of violent crimes, murders, which involve people who have had a rocky relationship with Lucy. The latest prostitute to get murdered, Alice Mitchell, had fought with Lucy before. The last person to visit with Alice was Calvin Jessup. I am confident that Jessup is the person who released his dogs on me."

"You are giving me a headache, Patrick."

"I am sorry, sir, but that is what we know."

"And you can't find anyone?"

"We are looking. Riley and I went to a place that Jessup frequents, but he wasn't there. Two thugs told us that Jessup was fearful of some men wanting to kill him. Riley and I set them straight."

"Spare me the details," Shipley said. "What of this Gardner girl?"

"Fifteen years old," Riley said. "The parents said she snuck out of her bedroom window."

"There is also a girl missing from Holy Trinity's orphanage, same age, bares a strong resemblance to Helen Gardner. I think the cases might be connected," I said.

"How come I never heard of this girl from Trinity?"

"It was not reported to the department. They asked me to privately look into her disappearance. I found very little."

"I don't approve of free lancing," Shipley said. His face was getting redder, if that was possible. "Let's follow these two cases as closely as we can. The situation with George Loftus is extremely disturbing. I assume he will turn up at some point."

I wasn't as confident at Shipley. "Is that all, sir."

"Not even close. The situation on the southside is very worrisome. You know the city has extra patrols out there. There is fear of a large uprising. To make matters worse Matthew Batholomew is giving a speech in the black section at eleven o'clock. I would like you and Riley to get out there to see what you can learn."

"What is his goal, Lieutenant?" Riley asked.

"I'm thinking that is he is going to try to rile up as many people as he can, get people to believe him so he can try and raise funds for his cause."

"I don't suppose his cause has dug up any leads on any of the murders down there?" I asked.

"He hasn't," Shipley said. "Have we?"

To date there was nothing new. The added patrols had been asking. Since the first hanging of James Jefferson, no one had seen or heard anything. "Not yet," I said.

"Then I think we should get to work."

• • •

Matthew Bartholomew's little speech was being held on the back of a trailer parked near an alley on 75th Street. Riley and I got there just as the speech was about to commence. It was still very cold and the snow on the ground had not melted; my feet were still cold. Bartholomew wore a very nice, heavy wool coat. His associates, Brand and Jennings stood behind him. Brand look tough; Jennings, the bookish looking secretary, looked to be freezing.

The gathered crowd, forty to fifty people, all black, stood huddled in front of the trailer. I saw Sam Fuller close to the trailer. Standing beside him was James Jefferson's mother. I had no idea what kind of speech Bartholomew was about to give, but the message must have gotten out that it was going to be important.

"My friends," Bartholomew started, "I want to thank you all for coming out. It is a cold and gloomy day here in Chicago and that is similar to the city's attitude towards the black community." He stopped for a moment and you could hear the murmuring from the black attendees, echoing his thoughts.

"Even as the black community grows, there is no attention from city hall or the police department. We have a crisis here and no one is paying attention. If a white boy of fifteen, a white girl of seven or a white grandmother was murdered, not murdered, but tortured, the city and the police would turn over every stone to find the killers. With the victims all being black, the city has turned a blind eye to you, your people." This time the murmuring wasn't so indistinguishable. Some of the men yelled out there support of the comments.

"We at the Chicago Negro League are doing our best to raise funds for the betterment of the community. Your section of the town is growing and you need a strong voice. We intend to be that voice. But my words today, and what we are trying to accomplish, won't take care of the immediate problem. What is needed today is action, action by you all. The police won't help you. Who will be the next victim? A child, a mother, another grandparent? You need to rise up and take action on our own. You need to rise up to the assailants who don't want you as neighbors. This city is as much yours as it is theirs. You must make sure that they know that."

There was an awful lot of cheering and loud supportive comments from the crowd, a mostly male crowd.

"Is he trying to get these people to give money to his organization?" Riley asked me.

"I don't think so. My thought is he is trying to get them to riot to get the city and the police to actually pay attention to them."

"Haven't we paid attention to the murders?" Riley asked.

"My thoughts only, but I think the department may not prioritize the murder of a black person."

Riley grunted. He still hadn't warmed to the idea of helping the blacks, but Loftus was nowhere to be seen.

Matthew Bartholomew came through the crowd and right at us. His two aides were right behind him. "I see the department has sent out two of its finest detectives. All of these murders and no idea who is behind them."

"Our foot patrols, which have been increased, are asking everyone they see if they know anything. No one heard or saw a thing," I said.

"Such a practiced answer," he said. "You're on the wrong side of the road, Detective. The answer to your questions lie with the Irish."

I passed on a comment to that. "Some interesting ideas that you had today."

"It's a matter of guidance. These people need some guidance and I am trying to give them some."

"It sounded to me like you were trying to incite them."

"I am trying to get them to take some action for themselves. Maybe if they stand up for themselves, raise their voices, the city will take notice."

"Just raise their voices, "I said. "I am only hoping their actions don't cause more damage."

He smiled at me and walked away, his two cronies not far behind.

I saw Sam Fuller and walked towards him. His look towards me was not friendly.

"Sam," I said, "a rather uplifting speech."

"I think Bartholomew speaks the truth."

"Meaning what?"

"Meaning we are overlooked and need to do something on our own. There is nothing that says these murders are over. We have to do something."

"Do you know what that is?"

He gave me a weary look. "Not at this time, Detective." He turned and walked away from me.

"What do we do from here, Patrick?" Riley asked.

"I'm afraid, not too much. I'm thinking the next action that we take will be after something else has happened. I don't think it will be something good."

•   •   •

When we got back to the precinct, the mystery of George Loftus had been partially solved. Culligan's was a good-sized tavern on the north end of the Levee. I knew the owner Jimmy Culligan very well. I knew that he ran about as legal a joint as you could down here. That's why I was surprised by the news that we got when we entered the front door.

"There's some trouble with Loftus," Desk Sergeant Coogan said.

"What kind of trouble?" I said.

"We got a call from Jimmy Culligan. He said Loftus came in there, boosted him about stolen Canadian whiskey, popped him in the face, and then robbed him of about three hundred dollars."

"When did this happen?"

"Later last night. Jimmy said he just felt good enough now to call it in."

Luckily, the sun had warmed things up a bit and melted the snow. We were able to make the six block walk in good time. My shoes were still damp from the morning.

Jimmy Culligan was a little over six feet tall and as skinny as a rail. He had his dark brown hair combed straight back which showed the knot above his left eye. The bump was a nice color of purple. He didn't smile at me when I came through the front door. "Your partner is a son of a bitch, Moses."

I got up close and took a good look at the bruising. "What did he hit you with?"

"Butt end of that Colt he carries. Wasn't no love tap, either. Who the fuck tore your face up?"

I let that comment go. "I'm sorry, Jimmy. Tell me what happened."

"Loftus came in here about eleven o'clock. Some big, lanky guy was with him. He asks me what I know about stolen Canadian whiskey. I told him the same thing I told him the last five times he asked me. I told him I knew nothing."

"How big was this big guy?"

"Big. Six and a half feet I'd say. Long, crooked nose. Didn't say anything. Just stood behind Loftus the whole time."

"George asked you about the whiskey?"

"Yeah. We had talked about it before on better days. I told him I didn't know anything about any stolen whiskey. I told him I never bought anything that I thought might be stolen."

"What did he do?"

"Look at this," he said pointing to the bump. "He came around the counter drew his gun and popped me on the head. Then he opened the cash register and took what was in there. I think it was about three hundred."

"Did you see him leave?"

"Couldn't. I was lying on my back and I thought for a minute I might pass out. He clocked me pretty good."

"Nobody in here?"

"Just a few at the end of the bar, but Loftus didn't care. He would have done it if the place was packed."

I shook my head. "Was he drunk?"

Jimmy shrugged. "Seemed kind of fine but agitated. Seemed like he was in a hurry."

"And this big guy didn't do anything?"

"Not much. Just stood there. Loftus did all of the dirty work."

"Shit," I said. I couldn't think of anything smarter to say.

"Is Loftus in some kind of trouble?" Jimmy asked. "I've known him a long time. We were friends, I thought. He wasn't close to himself."

I looked over at Riley, but he looked in shock. I didn't know how to answer that question. Loftus had clearly become disengaged from who he was.

"Jesus, Patrick," Riley said on the way back. "What the hell is going on with George? What the hell do we do?"

"I don't know. First I get word that he's with Lucy. Now he's buddies with Calvin Jessup. It seems like the three of them are in cahoots together."

"Maybe if we find one of them we can find all of them."

"Riley, that is a bright idea, but where the fuck are they?" This came out a little harsh. Riley's facial reaction told me he didn't care for my tone. We walked the rest of the way in silence.

•   •   •

Our conversation with Lieutenant Shipley was very short. He wasn't angry. He just seemed to slip into a phase of acceptance that I can't explain. How do you explain that a trusted colleague has suddenly changed to a life of crime? When I thought about Loftus it stunned me; it was unbelievable. Maybe Joan was right. This job could tear your insides out and change you. I could see it in George, Shipley and myself.

I tried hard the rest of the day to gather thoughts on all of my three cases. It was tough after the Loftus' news. When I say three cases, I now lumped Rebecca Tilson and Helen Gardner together. Both had gone missing; both were curly blondes with full figures and both had mentioned meeting new boyfriends. Helen had been killed in the same vicinity where Rebecca disappeared. I thought there was a strong connection.

When we talked about the situation on the southside, Shipley merely nodded his head. He listened while we told him about the Bartholomew speech; he made some notes on paper. He told us he had no more people to deploy to the area. He almost seemed to accept that there was going to be a blowup between the two sides. I thought so, too, but I was more interested in finding the killers. There wasn't much to go on in that regards.

When I thought of George Loftus, I could only come up with one solution. We had been asked to check out Lucy VonMara. What we had found was disturbing. It was looking like Lucy was a cold blooded killer. When she became upset with someone they ended up dead. Somehow George blocked all of that out and became enamored with her. Now he was in some sort of alliance with Lucy and Calvin Jessup. I was wondering where this was going and how it was going to end. I didn't like the possible outcomes.

One thing that nagged at me. Both Rebecca Tilson and Helen Gardner spoke of boyfriends. One boyfriend came to mind, Robert from The Crow's Nest. It wasn't a sure thing, by far, but it was something.

• • • • • • •

I knew the kid was responsible for taking out the garbage, so I set my self near the trash bins in back of the bar. A place like The Crow's Nest did a big business. There would be a lot of trash so I didn't think I'd have to wait long for Robert to show up. I wasn't alone waiting back there in the alley. Two rats the size of small cats walked past my feet like they didn't mind or care that I was there. I knew they weren't waiting for Robert, but the treats he tossed out. They didn't bother me.

My wait was less than a half hour. I saw the back door open and Robert emerged, carrying two large sacks of trash. He walked awkwardly towards me, struggling with the weight of the bags. The temperature outside had dipped and it was near freezing. I heard Robert swear. When he got close to the cans, I stepped out in front of him.

"Jesus, man," he said. "You damn near scared the hell out of me."

"Sorry," I said. "Need a word or two."

He eyed me suspiciously and tossed the bags into the cans. "I told you all I know and I didn't say anything to my pop."

"This is a different topic, a different girl I need to ask you about."

"I don't know every girl in the city."

"Probably not, but I'm interested in this one."

He didn't say anything at first. "Make it quick. We are very busy and my pop will be expecting me back there to help."

"The girl's name is Helen Gardner, looks like she could be a twin sister for Rebecca Tilson."

"I don't know anyone by that name," he said.

"You sure. She told a bunch of people that she had a new boyfriend, that is, before she went missing. I wouldn't want it to turn up that she was talking about you."

I could see him smile. "I don't think it will be since I have no idea who you are talking about."

I nodded. "I had to ask. We have two young girls, both blondes with curls, who have gone missing in this general area."

Again he smiled at me. "There are a lot of blondes in the city who have curls."

I got up real close to him. He took a step backwards. "But only two have gone missing recently and one has turned up dead. I'd better not find out that you knew this second girl."

"I've got to get back inside," he said. He turned and was gone.

I saw my two rat friends climb the bin and jump into the garbage. I turned and walked away.

I needed a drink. I was done for the day and felt I had accomplished nothing. My temples were tight. What I didn't want was another lecture from Joan. I knew how dangerous the job was. I also knew how frustrating and fruitless it could be. Yes, I needed a drink.

Cooper's was crowded. I didn't want any food so I sidled up to the bar. There was an open stool on the end. Kenny was tending bar. "You're not going to become a regular again, are you, Detective Moses?" Kenny had been a bad drunk, he told me one time. Working the bar was his challenge to stay away from the booze.

"I'm only planning on having one, Kenny, but make it a double."

He shook his head but poured the whiskey into a glass. He put the drink in front of me. "I saw your partner, yesterday."

I sipped the whiskey. "Riley?"

"No. I saw Loftus."

This stopped me. "He came in here?"

"Sat right about where you are sitting."

"You get a chance to talk with him?"

"Sure. Loftus and I get along fine."

"He have anything interesting to tell you?"

"Don't you work with him?"

I took another sip. "He hasn't been in to work in a few days. We're actually looking for him. Kind of worried, too."

"That makes sense now. He was talking about maybe getting out of police work and doing something else. He said he had a met a woman, a woman like he'd never met before."

"That seems to make sense with what we'd heard. Did he tell you where he was staying?"

"That's the other thing. He went on about trying to find something new to do, a fresh start. He said he dumped his apartment and was staying at the Alaska Hotel until he could figure out what he wanted to do. I asked him what he thought he might get into and he kind of laughed. He said he wished he knew."

Robbing bars didn't seem like a great career to be getting into. "Did he say if he was with this woman at the Alaska?"

"Didn't say. Just told me she was the biggest difference in his life in a long time."

Loftus had been down for a bit, I was told. His drinking was way up. He meets Lucy VonMara and she seems to bring some clarity to his life. He turns completely. The Hotel Alaska was less than a mile from Cooper's.

"You okay, Moses? You went away for a bit."

I tossed back the rest of the whiskey. "I'm good."

"I hope Loftus is okay. He seemed a little down."

I tossed money on the bar for the drink. "I'm going to try and find out." I turned and walked back out into the night.

·   ·   ·

The Hotel Alaska was a dumpy, three story place on Wabash near 22nd. The biggest story from the place was when the two ward aldermen paid vagrants a dollar each for their votes and let them stay at the Alaska for free for a couple of nights. I had only been in there one time; a frisky patron had gotten a little too aggressive with a prostitute and she stabbed him in the heart. When the police got there she said she hadn't meant to kill him.

The night clerk was dozing when I walked into the Alaska. He was sitting behind the reception counter, leaning back in his chair, drool sliding out of the side of his mouth. I gave the counter a hard rap and the kid popped up. My badge was now in his face.

"What'd I do?" he asked.

"Nothing yet, but I need your help."

He still wasn't quite awake and wiped sleep from his eyes and drool from his face. "What help?"

"I'm looking for three people. One is a good looking woman, busty, with black hair. One other is a very tall man, has a long crooked nose. The third is a little bigger than me, dark hair, wears nice suits."

He thought for a moment. Maybe they paid him off. My badge seemed to sway his thoughts. "Real tall guy is up there in room two-ten. The other two were staying here, but I think they left."

"They left?"

He shrugged. "They didn't tell me where they were going."

"Got a back-up key for two-ten?"

He reached behind him and grabbed a key from a little cubby hole on the wall. He gave it to me. "I'm not supposed to give these out."

"I won't tell anyone."

"What did they do?"

"Killed a few people, people who talked too much."

"I didn't tell you anything."

I turned and headed for the stairs. I drew my gun as I climbed to the second floor. With these three, in their current state of mind, I wanted to be ready. When I got to two-ten, I stopped. I remembered my former partner, Sam Walker, barging into a brothel room and getting half of his head blown off. I inserted the key quietly and turned it. The lock snapped and I pushed the door open. My gun was leading the way into the room. Being one-armed still was a big disadvantage.

The room was dark, but there was a little glow coming from an open window that showed a large body in the bed. I approached slowly. The body was turned away from me, but I could clearly see the back of Calvin Jessup's head. I wanted to just shoot the bastard, but I needed information from him. I gave him a not too gentle tap on the head with the revolver. Like the desk clerk, he popped up in a hurry.

"What? Who?" he said.

The little bit of light let me see his face. It was long and had a lot of skin to it. His nose was long and thin. This was where I aimed my revolver when I used it to smack him. "That's for sicking your dogs on me."

Blood started to ooze out of his nose and he used his sheet to stop it. He looked up at me or rather my gun barrel. "What do you want?" he said in a whiny voice. "You broke my damn nose."

"Where are Lucy and Loftus?"

"I don't know," he said. "They said they were leaving for a bit."

I pushed the gun barrel up against his forehead. "Where?"

"I don't know. They left earlier."

I kept the barrel there. "You and Loftus rob Culligan's?"

"That was Loftus. He said we could get some quick cash there."

"What about the murder at Heaven's Gate. The prostitute, Alice Mitchell, somebody cut her up pretty bad."

"I went upstairs with the girl," he said. "We had a little fun." He laughed. "Lucy told me to go out of the door on the second floor and leave it unlocked. She said she had some unfinished business with the girl. I had no idea she was going to kill her."

"Let me get this straight. You let Lucy into a brothel room, but you had no idea what she was up to. You also decided to let two big fucking dogs loose on me with the intent of tearing me apart. I'm not buying any of your story, Calvin. You'd better tell a different one. You're sounding an awful lot like an accomplice in one murder and the prime suspect in attempted murder. No judge is going to help you out much in these cases."

He wiped more blood from his nose. "What are you going to do?"

"Well, I could shoot you right here," I said. His eyes opened wide at that. "Or, if you help me, we can talk to the prosecutors about a lighter sentence. There is no way you're getting off with nothing."

"I had no idea what she was up to."

"Cut the bullshit. It's late and I want to go home. Give me something to help me out."

"Okay. They went to Cicero."

"Cicero. Why there?"

"Lucy was always talking about opening her own place. She thought Cicero might be that place. They went there to check on possible locations."

I nodded. "What's with her and Loftus?"

He laughed. "Man, he fell head over heels in love with her. He looks like he's floating when he walks next to her."

"And you?"

He paused for a moment. "I love Lucy, too, but she never loved me back. I was always there for her, but there was nothing in return. I guess I let her use me."

Stupidly, I felt sorry for the big lug. He had been duped by the beautiful Lucy VonMara. "Get up and get dressed. I'm going to take you into the 22nd for booking. Try anything stupid and I will shoot you in the head. Got it?"

"Yeah, I got it. I'm done doing anything stupid for Lucy."

He got dressed and we walked down the stairs together. I had the clerk call the station and a vehicle showed up to transport us back to the precinct. I got Jessup booked and into a downstairs cell. By the time I got home, Joan was fast asleep and I was wide awake. I was in the bed for a long time before I drifted off. I was being overwhelmed by my cases.

Chapter Eleven

It wasn't a riot that occurred late last night. It was an attack. The number of attackers varied depending on who you talked to, but the description of them was consistent. A large group of black hooded men came into the Irish area around midnight and attacked a group of twelve white men who were drinking at The Taproom, the bar where Whitey had been found beaten to death behind it.

The attackers came in through both the front and back doors, brandishing wooden clubs. Once inside the bar they began to pummel anyone in sight. There were no words spoken, no declarations. Their goal was to attack and maim as many people as they could. Of course, this was a revenge tactic. There was no doubt that it had been provoked by Matthew Bartholomew's speech. He had asked the black community to rise up. They had and the results were a one-sided onslaught.

If we needed further proof who the attackers were, we had it. One of the black hooded men was lying dead by the front door. He might have been the only casualty from that side; we'd never know. The owner of The Taproom, Danny Conlin, had shot this invader in the back. Someone had taken off his black hood, revealing a younger black man.

"It happened so damn fast," Conlin said. He had a large lump on the side of his head. "I was busy trying to make drinks when there was this sudden commotion. I looked up and they were coming in from the front and the back. They were incensed, swinging those clubs at any white head they could see. It was madness."

Riley and I had both been summoned out of bed. We looked around the bar. There were four dead white men on the floor. The story was pretty much the same for all of them. Depending on who hit them, they all had significant damage to their heads. Along with the dead bodies were overturned tables and chairs, broken glasses, and blood. A lot of blood.

"I turned my head and this one black bastard came right over the bar," Conlin said. "He swung his club at me and he got me pretty good. I went down and he must have thought I was out because he stepped right over me. It took me a while to come to, but I was able to pull myself up and get my gun. I looked over the bar just as they were starting to run for it. That was when I shot that piece of shit in the back."

"How many of them were there?" I asked.

"Twenty, thirty, at least," he said. "Crazy goddamn people."

We suggested that he might want to get over to Mercy to get the head checked, but he shook us off. "I been hit a lot worse than this. You know, the Army, and then running a bar for over twenty years. Seen some good ones."

There wasn't a whole lot more for the trained investigators to see. Riley and I took another look around the place. It was a shambles. A couple of ambulances had shown up to take out the bodies of dead. As the crew moved one of them onto a stretcher, I recognized the face of Bucky O'Neil, the hardware store owner. I wondered again if the rope used in the hangings had been purchased in his store. If he did know who made the purchase we'd never know now.

"Where to, Patrick?" Riley asked.

I exhaled deeply. I was tired, my temples ached and my vision was a little blurry. "It won't do us any good, but we'd better talk to Sam Fuller. We won't get any names, but I'm pretty sure he's got some knowledge of how this all started."

We made the short drive over to Sam Fuller's small house and knocked on the door. It was a cold November morning. There was no sun and thick clouds hung overhead. Could be rain soon or more snow. Sam opened the door, dressed in work clothes, and stepped out onto the porch with us. He closed the door behind him.

"No bullshit this time, Sam. Any idea who the people were that went into The Taproom last night and busted it up?"

"Don't know nothin about anything like that," he said, straight faced.

"Probably don't know anything about the dead, black man shot in the back, either?

His face showed a little grimace. "Ain't heard about anyone getting killed."

"Okay," I said. "I see where this goes. Your side makes a little visit to Irishtown and beats up and kills a few of theirs. They snatch somebody else and hang them or maybe they attack a large group of your people. Sounds like an awful pattern."

Sam stared at me. There was no response from him.

"So where does this all end, Sam? You all just going to keep on killing each other?"

He cocked his head to one side. "You tell me, Detective Moses. We didn't start any of this. We just want to live in peace, take care of ourselves, raise our families. We didn't want any of this. What are we supposed to do?"

He was right. They hadn't started any of this madness. What were they supposed to do? "It might be a good idea if you all stopped killing each other."

He looked at me as if I told him someone from the moon had come to visit. He laughed a bit, shook his head, and went back into his house, closing the door on us.

I left Riley behind to look into any information he could get about the bar attack while I returned to the precinct to report to Lieutenant Shipley. I didn't argue with Riley when he told me that was probably a waste of time. No one from either side of the neighborhoods was talking very much. There were vicious crimes being committed on both sides of the street and no one knew anything.

I wasn't expecting the building to be as quiet as it was when I returned, but I learned all of the uniforms were headed south to try and maintain control. I thought this was a waste of time as well. What happened last night was a coordinated attack; it wasn't the beginning of some larger uprising. While the cops were patrolling 63rd Street, I wondered who was guarding the Levee.

I went upstairs to see Shipley, but his door was closed. His little secretary, a middle-aged woman named Agnes was at her desk, but she looked busy. She barely saw me walk up. "What can I do for you, Detective?" she said.

"I was going to give Lieutenant Shipley an update on the events on the southside," I said.

She laughed and almost choked. "He doesn't need any updates. He's got every person in City Hall calling him. The Central Station won't leave him alone."

"That neighborhood is not really under our watch," I said.

She pointed a bony finger at me. "That is true, but your little unit was asked to find out what was going on and to come up with some sort of solution so that this kind of thing didn't happen."

Not really true, I thought. We were asked to investigate some hangings which turned into five murders. Shipley had been worried about a total outbreak, but we had never been asked to figure out a solution. "I'm here if Shipley wants to talk with me."

Another laugh. "I doubt he'll want to talk with anyone, but I will let him know."

I walked back down the stairs. It looked like Desk Sergeant Coogan was all alone, but I didn't want to talk with him. The other person I saw was Sister Theresa from Holy Trinity. She was looking at pictures on the wall. One of those pictures was of my late father. I had shot him dead on Christmas Day a couple of years ago.

She turned as I approached her and pointed to my father's picture. "He looks like you."

"That's my father. He used to do a lot of work for the two aldermen who run this ward."

"You must be proud to see his picture hanging in the building where you work every day."

I had grown to hate and despise the man. "We had a complicated relationship. He was my father, but I lived in the orphanage at Holy Trinity."

She smiled weakly. "I wondered about that, if it was your father."

"Like I said, complicated, but you didn't come here today to talk about my father."

"This is the emptiest I have ever seen this building."

"The uniforms have been sent to the southside where there is a bit of social unrest."

"The nice desk sergeant was telling me about that."

I wouldn't consider Coogan to be nice, but he was good with the general public. "It's a mess."

"I'm sorry, but I won't take up much of your time."

"I've got a little."

"It's about Father Corcoran, I was wondering if you had a chance to talk with him."

"I did. He denied anything about improper touching of anyone. I can't do a lot if there is nothing to back it up."

She nodded. "Nothing new in your search for Rebecca Tilson?"

"Not much, really." Other than finding a dead girl that looked like Rebecca there wasn't much and searching for her had been relegated to the bottom of my list.

"There's a very good chance that she has just run away. She wouldn't be the first orphan to just go."

That was a thought many shared, but when we found Helen Gardner my thoughts changed. I thought she might be dead. "That would seem to be a logical solution."

"But Father Corcoran keeps popping into my head. I just have this nagging suspicion that he knows something."

I rubbed my aching temples. "About Rebecca Tilson?"

"He's always leaving the building at night. I hear he is not wearing his collar and is in lay clothes."

I knew of some of his adventures, but not all of them. "Where do you think he goes?"

"I think he goes into the Levee to look for women. I think he has a problem, one that he can't control. I can't prove any of this, but there are rumors. It's not something you can confront someone about."

I had confronted him. I didn't know if he would listen. "What would you like me to do?"

"It might be a silly request, maybe a bad idea, but could you follow him?"

"Follow him? What night would I know to follow him?"

"He told one of the other nuns that he would be visiting some families throughout the area tomorrow night and that he might not be up the following day until later. I think he is heading for the Levee District."

I nodded slowly. "I can keep a watch on him tomorrow. What do you intend to do if I find him doing something he shouldn't be doing?"

She smiled again. "I intend to report him to the Diocese."

I didn't smile, but I shared her thoughts. Father Corcoran had a problem. I knew others with the same problem, but they weren't priests.

•   •   •

We had time to send a telegram to the police department in Cicero. We asked them to look for a tall woman, bosomy, with dark, black hair. Her companion was tall, over six feet, also with dark hair. He was probably armed. I didn't want to say armed and dangerous. This was Loftus I was talking about and I really hoped he hadn't fallen into completely evil ways. We told Cicero that these two might be looking for a location to open a brothel. They responded that they would keep an eye out for the pair. I wasn't encouraged by their response.

Riley had returned from the southside with very little to report. The dead black man at The Taproom was named William Thomas. His family indicated that they had no idea where he was going when he went the night before. He had a habit of stopping by a local tavern. He had been at the speech given by Matthew Bartholomew and had become angry after it. His family was not surprised that he had entered the fray; he often fought for being treated equally. They were asked if they had any idea who he might have been with. The answer was a firm no.

A young girl by the name of Mary Ellen Bradley had come into the station with her parents. She said she wanted to talk with someone about what happened to Helen Gardner. Desk Sergeant Coogan told them that the detectives that were handling the case were out. He got all of her information and told them they would get a visit at their home shortly. I gave Riley a little time to catch up on things and then we would head out to see her.

There was a note on my desk that Harold Pinter wanted to see me in his little basement laboratory. I wanted to talk with Calvin Jessup anyway so I headed downstairs to speak with Harold first. I hadn't heard a word from Shipley. I imagined he was still getting a barrage of questions from City Hall and also the Central Station. He might be answering them all afternoon.

I hadn't spoken to Harold in a while. I knew there were always crimes in the Levee that required a criminologist like him to be involved. We were relying more on physical evidence and Harold was superb in analyzing it. I wondered what he had that he wanted to talk with me about. I found him at his desk, staring up at a picture that he held slightly above his head.

"Look better up there than on your desk?" I asked.

He put the picture down on his desk. "A little better light up there, Patrick. I'm glad you stopped by to see me. This is interesting. I think it will help you with the murder of Helen Gardner."

I sat down in the extra chair that Harold had. "Right now, we need all of the help we can get."

"There is no doubt that Helen was murdered by strangulation. The scarf that was around her neck was pulled so tightly that it broke the skin on her neck, but there was something else."

I shifted a bit on the chair. Harold had a way with stories, telling them slowly, when you really wanted to get the facts quickly.

"On the left side of her chin, I noticed some scratches above the neck. The neck had some bruising which I thought could be from the fingers of someone choking her."

"What about the scratches?"

"Patience, Patrick," he said. "I believe the scratches came from a ring that the assailant was wearing on his right hand. As he choked Helen the ring rubbed against her chin causing the scratches."

"You're sure the killer is a he?"

He shrugged. "Just a guess."

"Any special pattern to the scratches?"

"No pattern, but there were quite a few, some were deeper than others. I'd say that this ring has a sharp edge. I'd say find a man with a ring with a sharp edge and you may have your killer."

"Easier said than done."

He laughed. "I can only provide you with information that might lead you to your killers, not find them for you. That is your job."

I nodded. It was certainly a job that I wasn't relishing at the moment.

· · ·

Calvin Jessup was locked up in one of the cells that was on the other side of the basement. He was sitting on his small cot, looking down at the floor. The jailer opened the door for me and I walked in. Jessup sat up and looked at me. "The lawyer the city sent me said I shouldn't talk to you anymore," he said. His crooked nose was swollen and turning colors.

"I thought we were friends."

He failed to see the humor in my comment and didn't smile. "What do you want?"

"Your lawyer is trying to protect you. You were the one who let the dogs loose on me, attempted murder. You left the second story door open for Lucy to get in, accomplice to a murder. Those are some serious charges. You could be spending a long time at County. It's not that great a place."

"Moses, what do you want?"

"We sent a telegram to the Cicero Police for help with finding Lucy and Loftus. They haven't gotten back to us with anything yet. I am not too confident they will."

"That's where they told me they were going."

"I don't doubt that but were they planning on staying?"

"They said they'd be gone a couple of days."

"They completely checked out of the Alaska. Where else might they be staying?"

"You can really help me with my charges?"

I thought of Prosecutor Higgins. I wasn't sure, but it was worth a try. "I think I can."

"I don't know very much."

"You loved Lucy, didn't you?"

A big tear ran out of Jessup's left eye and ran down his face. "I still love her."

"But she favors Loftus?"

He wiped at the tear. "I guess so."

"So why help them? Lucy is not here helping you now and I don't think she will if she comes back."

The poor man looked broken. He knew he was going to jail for a long time. "There's a small house on 44th Street. Can't miss it. It's got an oak in front of it that was hit by lightning. The trunk is all black from the scorching it got. Lucy has a key to the place, don't ask me how. She goes there sometimes to hide out. Quiet time she calls it. If and when they come back, I think she might go there."

"44th Street?"

"About a mile west of the lake."

"I'll talk with the prosecutor," I said.

He looked up at me. His eyes were swollen and wet. "Tell him I helped you, Moses."

"I will," I said. I turned and left the cell.

•   •   •

Mary Ellen Bradley and her family lived in a small house just north of Chicago Avenue. It was getting later in the day, and colder, so it took our coach a while to get there. Riley looked tired, lighting a cigarette, but tossing it out of the cab after a drag or two.

"What's got you?" I asked.

"Chasing clues and leads in these cases is like my stupid dog chasing his tail. We may get close, but we're never going to catch it."

"On the southside, somebody knows something on both sides of the street, but everyone is covering up everything."

"And this thing with Loftus and Lucy," he said, "Loftus has lost his mind."

"Seems that way. Maybe the Cicero Police can tell us something or maybe they'll show up at this house Jessup mentioned."

"Or maybe they'll just come into the station and turn themselves in."

"Maybe," I said. "I'm hoping that Mary Ellen Bradley can tell us a little bit about why Helen Gardner got murdered."

"It would be nice to get one solid lead on something. Any news on your missing orphan girl?"

There was a chance that Rebecca Tilson was gone. The only thing that was tugging me in the other direction was her resemblance to Helen Gardner. "Right now, nothing. She may have taken off."

"You were an orphan, but you stayed."

"I was, but I was getting some preferential treatment and I liked the people there."

"Maybe she didn't," Riley said. He lit another smoke.

"That's my guess."

•   •   •

Mary Ellen Bradley was a very small fifteen year old. She had curly red hair and wore eyeglasses that looked too big for her face. It was obvious to us that she was very nervous that we were in her house. She sat on a sofa between her two parents.

"I don't want you to be scared about talking to us," I said. "We are just trying to find out what happened to Helen. Anything you might be able to tell us could help."

She kept her eyes down, not looking at us. She didn't respond at all.

"You came into the precinct to tell us something. Can you help us out a little, Mary Ellen?"

"Tell the detectives what you remember," her father said.

Her head came up, but she was not looking at us. She seemed to be looking at a spot beyond us. "Helen stopped coming around a little after school. We used to get together a lot."

"Do you know where she was going?" I asked.

She shook her head. "I don't know," she said.

This confused me. "But you knew something?"

"I don't know exactly where she went, but I knew she had met someone, a boy. She told me about him, but not where they met up."

"Okay. What can you tell me about this boy?"

She finally looked right at me. "I don't know much about him, but he was older. She told me she had snuck out at night a few times to meet him."

That confirmed what Helen's parents had said about her sneaking out. "What about the boy?"

"She told me his name was Ronny. She said he was older, out of school and that he had a job. I asked her what he looked like and she told me he was taller and had this brown hair that kept falling over his face."

"You sure she said Ronny?"

She looked at me like I was stupid. "I heard her say his name on numerous occasions. She said Ronny."

"How long was she seeing this boy?"

She thought for a moment. "I'd say a couple of months, maybe a little less. She started up with him when school started for the fall."

I thought about Robert from The Crow's Nest. Could Robert, who might be called Robby, go by another name such as Ronny. He had longer brown hair that he kept brushing out of his face. The habit annoyed me. "Did Helen tell you what kind of job this Ronny had?"

She shook her head again. "Not exactly, only that he worked somewhere for his father."

My stomach tightened. "Nothing more you remember?" I asked.

She started to cry a bit. "Helen told me she thought she loved this Ronny. She was starting to see him a lot. She wasn't paying much attention to anything else. I told her to be careful, but she only laughed at me. She told me she thought I was jealous because I didn't have a boyfriend. We argued and she told me to mind my own business. That was our last talk. She didn't listen and look what happened."

The poor kid went into a crying fit. Her mother put her arm around her and tried to console her, but I could see that this was going to be useless. The father looked at me, a helpless look. Riley and I let ourselves out the front door to the waiting coach.

Riley lit a cigarette as the coach headed back to the precinct. "Gonna be hard to find one boy named Ronny in this city," he said. "If he was telling Helen Gardner his real name."

I thought of Robert. "I wonder about that."

"Where to? It's getting late."

"Let's check out the house on 44th that Jessup told me about. Maybe we can get an idea where Loftus and Lucy are."

"Nothing back from Cicero, I take it?"

"Nothing yet."

• • • •

The house wasn't much, a one story frame structure with a huge oak tree in the front yard. A good portion of the tree had been damaged by lightning. On the left side of the house was a vacant lot that looked like a lot of junk had been dumped there. On the right, the closest house was about a hundred yards away. We had gone back to the precinct and gotten a vehicle to make the drive to the house. We parked down the street hoping we would not be seen. It didn't seem like that was a problem.

"Place looks dark," Riley said. "Doesn't look like anybody's in there."

"Can't hurt to look," I said. I got out of the car and approached the house. The street was quiet. I could hear my feet crunching fallen leaves.

"You think this is a good idea, Patrick?"

"Not really, but I'm trying to find them, not hide from them. I'll take the front. You go around back."

There were only a couple of steps that led up to the small porch fronting the place. I drew my gun and walked the stairs as Riley went around in back. Loftus' actions during the bar robbery made me think he might be a bit unhinged. I knew he would shoot anything that came through the door uninvited. My heartbeat quickened. Riley was right. This might not be a great idea.

I thought going through the door quietly might lead to me getting a hole in my head. What I decided to do was try and the door, and if was open, push it inward very hard, making as much noise as I could. There would either be shooting or not.

I placed my hand on the doorknob and it turned easily in my hand. I gave a short push and the door moved inward. I gave it a hard push, ducked to the left and knelt quickly. There was nothing. There was no shooting or noise of anyone moving about in the house. I got up and stepped through the door. In the fading light of the day I could see the house had one main room, a kitchen area, bedroom and a small bath. I moved to the back and opened the door. Riley joined me in the house.

"Nobody home?" he asked.

"Just us," I said.

I looked about the main room. An old sofa and two chairs seemed to be the highlights. The bedroom had a small bed, completely made, and a dresser. There was nothing in it.

"This place looks like there hasn't been anyone in it for a while," Riley said.

I couldn't disagree. "Lucy and Loftus know they're on the run. I doubt they are setting up home anywhere. I think they are traveling with all the clothes they need and that's it."

"Jessup said Lucy comes to this house?"

"That's what he said. A little away from the heart of the city."

"We can have a younger cop watch the place."

I nodded. "You and I can't sit here all day and watch the joint. We'll talk to Shipley in the morning."

"I'm hungry, Patrick, and the wife will be looking for me."

I thought of Joan. I thought it might be a good idea to get home early as well. "Let's get out of here."

•   •   •

Joan had finished eating her dinner by the time that I got home. My meal was waiting for me as was a copy of the day's *Chicago Tribune*. I quietly ate my dinner alone; Joan was doing something

179

in the bedroom. She came out just as I was about to open the paper.

"Would you like some coffee?" she asked.

I never drank coffee in the evening. "No. Thanks," I said.

"I know you've been having a rough few days," she continued. "I know you are involved in several bad cases."

I pushed the paper aside. "We are always involved in bad cases. What I have been going though recently is no different from before."

She bit her lip. She was starting to show a bit more. Her face had a nice glow to it. "I was wondering if you'd given any thought to what I asked of you?"

This caught me a little off guard. I tried to pay attention to everything she said at the end of the long days, but sometimes my mind wandered to the cases. I had to be honest here. "What exactly did you ask of me?"

She let out a sigh. "When we talked about our future together and we discussed how dangerous your job was."

"I remember the discussion, but I don't remember you asking me to do anything."

"You may be a great detective, but you are not really that smart."

This hurt a bit, but I held my temper. "I know what I do is dangerous and I told you that I always take precautions before I go rushing into anything. I'm trying to be as safe as I can."

"Then you haven't really considered what I asked you?"

I felt my temples tighten. "We'll have to stop talking in riddles. What exactly are you asking me to do?"

"The sooner the better, I would like you to quit the force. I would like you to be a long term father, not one the child never knows."

We had had this discussion. I thought I was clear about what I could do and couldn't do. I was a cop. That was about it. "I haven't really given it much thought. The cases are taking up a lot of my time."

"But you'll consider it, for me?" she said quickly.

I didn't want to lie. I didn't want to say something that I'd have to cover up later on. I really didn't want to say anything, so I didn't. I'm sure I looked like a mute, staring at her.

"That's what I thought," she said. She turned away from me and walked into the bedroom, closing the door quietly behind her.

My temples tightened even more and I saw the dancing, flashing lights in my eyes. I tried to read the front of the paper, but the words were blurry. I closed my eyes and held them tightly closed for a moment. When I opened them things were a little clearer with my vision. What was not clear to me was what was going on with Joan. She wanted me to quit the force; that was the farthest thing from my mind. We were at an impasse.

Chapter Twelve

"We received a telegram from Cicero last night," Shipley said. He looked tired with dark circles under his eyes.

He didn't elaborate so I spoke up. "Was there anything in it that would help us?"

He grabbed a piece of paper from the top of his desk and read it quietly. "Two people fitting Loftus' and Lucy VonMara's description got into a bit of an altercation at a tavern down there. Looks like a fight. They were told to get out of town. They were never charged or arrested."

"So I guess that means they are headed back here?"

"That's a good guess, Moses, but who knows? I saw your request that we put a man on that house on 44th. Right now, we are so thin, I can't put anyone out there fulltime, but we can have someone swing by there nightly."

I wasn't going to argue with him on that point. He seemed so beat up. "This Helen Gardner murder, she had a boyfriend who she said was called Ronny. We're going to try and find him, but we don't' know a whole lot."

"That's a sad story. What was this girl, fifteen years old? Who does these kind of things?"

Shipley had been a cop for longer than me. He had been in the Levee District for a long time now. He knew the types of evil that we dealt with on a daily basis. I didn't feel any need to respond.

"So, Moses, what is going to happen on the southside? Are the Irish and the blacks going to have a full scale war and just keep killing each other?"

"It's a very sad situation. It's not one person killing someone. It's an organized effort on both sides to inflict pain on the other. I'm going to say the Irish started this all with the hangings, but now the blacks have gained a foothold and have fought back."

A weak smile crossed his face. "And no end in sight?"

"I can't answer that."

"We have a lot of foot cops patrolling down there, but not enough. We don't know where the next altercation will take place. We're doing all we can, right?"

It was apparent that none of Shipley's bosses were agreeing with this assessment. "I'm not sure what more we can do. Things happen, but nobody hears or sees anything."

"This is an endless battle in this city and especially the Levee. Crime doesn't stop. We figure one case out and a new one pops up the next day. It's tiring."

"Yes, it is," I said.

He stared at me for a moment. "Find Loftus and Lucy VonMara, find the killer of Helen Gardner. Let's at least clear those two cases. The southside may have to settle on its own. I don't see that one having a simple resolution."

I nodded. "I agree."

"Get me something, Moses."

I knew the little meeting was over. I didn't know if the Central Station had given Shipley an ultimatum, but it was clear he was near the end of his rope. He needed some good news and quickly.

Riley and I made the drive to the house on 44th again. This time is was broad daylight. The sun was shining, but it was cold. We stayed down the street from the house for a while. There was no sign of another vehicle in sight. If Loftus and Lucy had returned from Cicero they hadn't come back to the house. The drab house with the half-burnt tree in the front yard looked deserted.

"They aren't here, Patrick," Riley said. We had been sitting quietly, both smoking slowly.

"They've got to come back," I said.

"Maybe. Maybe they just took off. Loftus has to know we are looking for him; you said Lucy wasn't that dumb either. Maybe they just said the heat was too hot in Chicago and they went away.

I had finally taken the sling off my bad arm; it felt stiff. "Maybe," I said. I flicked the cigarette butt out the window. "Let's go."

We drove south, not more than a couple of miles. We drove up 63rd and then went over to 75th. On either side of the road, there wasn't much to see. Not that many people were out, and those that were didn't look very menacing. We went by Cullen's. Cleanup was still underway, but the place was closed for business.

"Out of respect," Riley said.

"The neighborhood is very quiet."

"Think about it. Four of your friends and neighbors had their heads bashed in. They are all in mourning."

"Yeah," I said. "That and probably planning their next move."

"Seemed quiet on the black side of town, too."

"They know something bad is coming down the road. All they can do is wait."

Riley spit out of the open window. "It's a sad situation."

I didn't say anything at first. "What about Helen Gardner?"

"Her little friend said she was sneaking out to see a boy named Ronny. We've just got to find Ronny."

I thought of Robert, maybe a Robby. Couldn't be, I thought. "Let's head on back in. Lucy and Loftus aren't back; nothing's going to happen down here today and we have no idea who or where Ronny is."

"What do we tell Shipley if he asks?"

My temples tightened a notch. "The truth, I guess. We are light on facts."

. . .

Late in the afternoon a young man approached my desk. He had sandy colored hair and clear dimples on his face. He looked like he was about college age. The suit he wore didn't fit him very well. He looked nervous.

"You look like you might be lost," I said.

He smiled. "I don't think so. I'm looking for Detective Moses. That's you, right?"

Now he had my attention. "That would be me. Who are you?"

He sat down in the chair opposite my desk. "My name is Carl Manning. I was sent here by downtown."

Downtown being the Central Station. "And why would downtown send you to see me?"

"They told me you needed me for a surveillance detail."

For a minute, I was confused. "Some house near the StockYards," he said.

The Lucy/Loftus house. "It's not just a house, but a house where a murdering prostitute is alleged to hang out in."

"A murderer?"

"Pretty sure, but this should be an easy assignment. I want you to drive up to the place, park down 44th a bit and watch for any activity in the house. If you see movement inside or lights going on you need to get to a call box and contact the 22nd right away. They can reach me and Detective O'Donnell. You don't need to do anything else."

Carl swallowed hard. "But she is a killer?"

"Like I said, we are pretty sure. She is considered very dangerous. Just keep watch and report anything you see. Do not approach the house or them if you see something."

"I should sit in an automobile?"

"You can get one out back. Sign it out to me. You can drive, right?"

"Yes, sir."

"Knock that off. It's Patrick or Moses."

Okay, Detective."

I smiled. "Relax, Carl. Get the vehicle and head out there about seven when it is nice and dark. Find a good place to watch the place and do what I told you. That's it."

"I was told this detail could go on for several nights?"

"It could. We have no guarantee they will be there tonight or at all. We are just trying to find them."

He nodded. "I hear her partner is a rogue cop."

It bothered me when the kid said that about Loftus. George Loftus had saved my life before. "He's a good cop. Something happened to set him off course."

"Is he supposed to be dangerous, too?"

I thought of the tavern robbery. "Yes, he is."

•   •   •   •   •

I had mentioned earlier about my disdain for surveillance. I had no idea what time Father Corcoran was supposed to leave Holy

Trinity or if he was going out at all. I got a carriage and told the driver that we would pull up in front of an entrance to the orphanage and wait for a bit. The driver didn't care as long as he was paid. We got there at seven-thirty; I thought of Carl Manning, watching the house on 44th. Both of us were probably in for a long night of nothing.

It got closer to eight o'clock when I saw another carriage pull up in front of the orphanage. This cab waited for over ten minutes before a figure headed out of the front entrance and got into the cab. The entrance was well lit. The figure was Father Richard Corcoran.

"Follow that carriage," I told my driver.

"Whatever you say, Detective."

We followed the cab for several blocks where it turned on Clark Street. It was headed south towards the Levee District. "They're headed towards the Levee," I said.

"Streets are going to get more crowded down there."

"Just don't lose him."

The streets did get more crowded as we followed slowly behind Corcoran's carriage. At 20th Street the cab turned left and pulled up in front of a brothel called Deliverance. We were down the street with a good view. There was a wait of several minutes before Corcoran got out of the cab and entered the brothel.

"Looks like he's going to be busy for a while," my driver said. "You want to wait or get out to watch."

"Don't' be a wise guy," I said, but the question was valid. Should I get out and enter the brothel or stay back here. I couldn't catch Corcoran red-handed if I waited in the carriage.

"The other cab ain't leaving," the driver said.

"Waiting for him?" I said.

"Could be. Could be just sitting, waiting for another fare."

I waited in the cab another five minutes and got my answer. Corcoran came down the brothel stairs holding the hand of a woman. He helped her up the steps into their carriage and he got in on the other side.

"I've got them," my driver said.

We followed closely as the cab turned north on Dearborn and headed back in the direction of Holy Trinity.

"Think he's taking her to the chapel?" my driver asked.

"Doubt it," I said. Where was he taking this woman?

The cab in front of us turned west on 12th Street. It wasn't in any hurry. It plodded along, the dumb horse dragging it at a leisurely pace. My heart was racing. Something was up. I saw that we were in the neighborhood of The Crow's Nest where Robert worked. The carriage in front of us pulled past it; the place looked crowded. It went for another mile up 12th and turned on a residential street. Another few streets and it turned down an alley. This spot was equidistant between The Crow's Nest and where Helen Gardner had been found. Halfway down the alley it stopped by what looked like an old carriage barn. We waited back, looking to see what happened. Corcoran soon got out of the cab and opened the door on the other side of it. He helped the woman out of the cab, holding her hand. He led her into a side door to the barn. The carriage they were in pulled away.

"Now it looks like they are going to stay there for a while," my driver said.

"Let me out here," I said after ten minutes

"Two dollars," he said.

I paid him and he pulled out of the alley, leaving me alone. I took a deep breath and approached the building. It looked to be lit inside by some lamps. I waited for another five minutes or so but heard nothing. My imagination was running free. What was going on. I felt my temples tighten. I didn't need the blurry eyes to kick in. I needed to make a move. Inside the garage, the woman screamed.

I drew my revolver and pushed the door open. I had been right about the lighting; two kerosene lamps glowed in corners of the small building. The images I saw blurred as I tried to focus my vision. There was a busty blonde woman tied to a large table in the center of the room. Not only blonde, but blonde and curly. She was completely nude. Her arms and legs were tied to large nails at the corners of the table. A ligature was tied around her neck. This piece of rope was being held and tightened by Father Thomas Corcoran. It was hard to tell he was a priest. He had ditched all of his clothing. His eyes were bulging; a gleam of sweat covered his face. On his right hand, the one holding the ligature, a large ring reflected off of the lighting.

I shifted my gaze to the corner of the room to my left. Robert was there sitting quietly. He, too, wore a trance like look as he watched the ritual being performed in front of him. For a moment it seemed like neither man noticed that I had barged into the barn. They were both still in their trances, tormenting the young woman. This threw me for a moment. I was at a loss for words. After all, Corcoran was a priest.

Corcoran turned towards me finally; the glaze on his face had gone away. "You are interrupting our service here," he said.

"Service?" I said.

"I am helping this young woman get to God. She needed redemption. I am providing a quicker path for her."

This wasn't real, I thought. The man was crazy. "Untie her," I said. "Now."

He smiled. "Detective Moses, you were raised by us. You are one of us. You know you shouldn't interfere with God's work."

"This is more like the work of the devil. Untie that woman. Your little game of playing the redeemer is over."

He smiled and pulled the ligature tighter. The woman squirmed on the table. She was struggling to breathe. Her supply of air was being cut off.

I pointed the gun at Corcoran. "Father Corcoran, one last chance. Do as I say or I'm going to shoot you."

He smiled again as that strange glow covered his face again. His eyes seemed to roll back. "Robert, now," was all he said.

Out of the corner of my eye I saw the large frame of Robert come out of his chair and start for me. Luckily he was a good ten feet away. I turned quickly and shot him in the chest, knocking him straight back. He spun away, holding his chest and hit the dirt floor hard. I pivoted on Corcoran. The priest seemed to wake up at the gun shot. He turned to me as I approached him. He looked stunned.

"You have killed an angel of God," he said. He pulled tighter on the rope; the woman on the table gurgled a choked breath.

He was out of reality; he wasn't there. I swung the revolver hard and got him on the top of the head. Now his eyes really rolled back as he collapsed to the floor. He was out cold.

I moved over to check on Robert. I rolled him on his back. He was breathing shallowly, but he was alive. I wasn't sure for how long. I moved back to the table and loosened the ligature on the choking woman. When I succeeded she choked hard a few times, gasping for air. I took the rope from the ligature and tied Corcoran to the table, securing his hands behind his back. He wasn't going anywhere.

The woman sat up on the table. She was rubbing her neck where the rope had cut into her. She looked at me, eyes wide, not sure what was going to happen next.

"I'm a police detective," I said. "You are safe."

"He said we were going to a private party," she said with a raspy voice. "It was my night off. He promised me good money."

I found her clothes and tossed them to her. "Get dressed," I said. "We've got to get someone to help us."

•   •   •

It took a while, but I was able to find someone who helped us track down a carriage and a police vehicle. An ambulance was called for Robert who was taken to Mercy Hospital. I rode with the shaking prostitute back to the 22nd. We put her in a meeting room with a cup of coffee. Once she settled down she would have to give a full statement of what happened to her. Being told you were going to a private party did not include being tied to a table and slowly choked to death.

I wandered down to the cell where Father Corcoran was being held. Sister Theresa did not have to worry about going to the Diocese about him. His career as a priest was over. What I wanted to find out was information about two other young women who had gone missing or were murdered. I knew that he knew something about both of them.

Corcoran was sitting on a cot, looking off into the space in front of him. His pale face lacked color. I noticed the lay clothes he wore, thinking he'd never see the white collar again. The knot on the side of the head where I had hit him was purple in color. It was the only color I saw.

"I need some answers," I said. "Don't lie to me or shift blame to anyone. It won't help you now."

He looked up at me. His eyes were a blurry red. I noticed he was still wearing the heavy ring. It had a jagged edge that had cut into the chin of Helen Gardner. "What would you like to know?"

"I'd like to know about Rebecca Tilson and Helen Gardner."

He laughed a bit. "Pretty girls, friendly, too friendly. These girls were promiscuous. They had no moral understanding. We were giving them the proper cleansing before releasing them to God."

I shook my head. "Where is Rebecca?"

He stared at me for a moment. "There is an empty field north of the carriage barn. She is buried there."

Now I nodded slowly. "But you went asking about her at a local brothel and casino."

"Not at all. I went looking for a woman who looked like Rebecca, a blonde with curls, the promiscuous type. That was what I always went looking for."

That made sense. All three women that we knew about had fit the same physical description. "Why was Helen taken to that stand of bushes? It wasn't that close to the garage."

"Robert and I talked. The lot was too close to bury two bodies there. We decided to take that poor girl further away."

"And what was Robert's role in this?"

"That's obvious isn't it?"

"I don't think so. I'm not following your logic."

He shook his head this time. "Robert was a confessor and a convert."

"You're going to have to explain that a little better."

"I had told you that he had been accused of coming onto some of our girls in a less than normal fashion. I heard his confession and admission of the sins he committed. He agreed to let me know if there were bad girls or women out there. He agreed that some of these girls needed to be released to God early. Both Rebecca and Helen had come into contact with Robert and had come onto him rather strongly. He contacted me and it was decided these girls needed the cleansing. He was able to get them to come along where we could secure them in the carriage barn."

"Once they were secured, did he have anything to do with their torture?"

He winced. "No torture, Detective Moses. Call it enlightenment. Call it what you like, but Robert took no part in anything once he lured the girls in."

I thought of Robert as a young man with problems who had been duped by a priest peddling some sort of religion to quell his own sick thirst. I thought of Corcoran as a sadistic murderer.

"God may not have the best view of you Detective Moses since you have stopped our program of cleansing."

"I'll have to ask him what his view of me is if I ever get a chance to meet him. You, on the other hand, will get no chance. You will be meeting Satan, and not soon enough. I am sure you will be a celebrated tenant of Hell."

It was nearly ten when I got upstairs. I couldn't believe how tense I was. My fingers were tingling. I was surprised Coogan was at the desk. A few people were milling about the front lobby.

"Done with your priest, Moses?" he asked.

"I'm done until the judge wants to see me."

"His little friend, the kid Robert, died at Mercy. Sounds like he wasn't much of a loss either."

I disagreed. Robert was young and misguided. Probably not too smart, either. I wasn't feeling great about his death.

"O'Donnell is on his way in," Coogan said. "There's been a fire on the southside, on 78th Street. A black church. Multiple casualties out there. You and Riley need to get out there."

I sat down on a hard wooden bench. My temples tightened and the flashing lights came back to my eyes. I put my face into my hands and took a deep breath. A long night was about to become much longer.

"You okay, Moses," Coogan asked?

"No, Coogan. I'm never really okay."

Coogan came out from behind the desk, holding a small bottle of whiskey. He offered it to me. I took a swig and felt my tension subside a bit. He patted me on the shoulder and went back to his post.

•　　•　　•

The church was small and looked to have once been white in color. The flames and the smoke had turned it black for the most part. When we got there the firemen had just finished putting out the remaining flames. The church had been burning for over an hour. The firefighters who had been at the scene had worked tirelessly to put the damn thing out. It didn't help that the building was all wood. The word tinderbox was mentioned.

"I heard there were casualties," I said to a Fire Captain. He looked at me, his face blackened by smoked and grunted. He pointed his finger towards a small, grassy lot next to the church.

I walked over there with Riley trailing behind me. There, lined up neatly, were nine sheet covered bodies. I could tell from the size and shape that some of the bodies were children.

"Jesus," Riley said.

A police chaplain was there. I'd met him before but had forgotten his name. He turned towards us. "They never had a chance," he said.

"What do you mean?" I asked.

He pointed to a pile of ropes on the ground. It looked like they had been cut into different sized sections. "Those were used the secure both the front and back doors, from the outside. Whoever started the fire then tossed bottles, filled with kerosene, and lit at the top through the windows. The bottles more than likely exploded, covering everyone with liquid flames. Between the flames and the smoke people couldn't find their way out. Some eventually got to the windows and busted their way out. They lived. Any others didn't."

"This was murder?" Riley said dumbly.

"On a grand scale," the chaplain said.

"Nine people," I said. "Nine more murders. When will this end?"

"Insanity," was all Riley could say. "What can we do, Patrick?"

What could we do? It was getting very late and it was dark and cold. There was a group of people standing across the street. They were being held back by a squad of patrolmen. The number was twenty or thirty. They were there to check on the bodies under the sheets. If they saw anything they would have told the cops who were standing by. My guess was nobody had heard or seen anything. "Let's head back in until morning. We're not going to learn a damn thing out here tonight."

"Insanity," Riley repeated.

•   •   •

The area around the Stock Yards always gave me nightmares. I found Eleanor Winter, slashed to death, near Bubbly Creek. We had also killed Arnold Perry and his partner in an old house while investigating Rupert Finch. Now I had asked a young fresh-faced kid to sit on a house where Lucy VonMara and George Loftus were supposed to hang out. I wondered what was going on at the house.

"We'd better check on Carl Manning since we are not that far away, "I said.

Riley was clearly rattled by the church fire; he was smoking cigarettes at a brisk pace. "Who the hell is Carl Manning?"

"The kid they sent me to watch the house where Lucy and Loftus hang out."

"Got to be having a better night than us."

It was only a couple of miles to 44th Street. The drive took less than five minutes. We approached the street from the side from which Carl was supposed to be watching from. We saw his automobile, facing towards the house. I could see lights on in the house.

"They're in the house," Riley said.

"Someone is."

I pulled up close to Carl's vehicle. The lights on our auto hadn't gotten him to step out of the vehicle. I turned the car off and got out. I couldn't see anybody in the other car. When I got close, I could see Carl slumped over in his seat. I thought he was asleep. I opened his door and he didn't move. I poked him, nothing. I lit a match and hovered it over his face. There was a large caliber bullet hole in the side of his head. Some of his brains were spread across the seat and the far side of the car. I stepped back.

"He's dead," I said. A wave of tension went through my body.

"Son of a bitch," Riley said. "They killed him and they're still in that house?"

I drew my gun. "Let's go see."

I started towards the house. I realized Riley wasn't behind me. He hadn't left Carl's auto.

"Are you coming?" I said.

"I've got a wife and four kids, Patrick. Those two are crazy. I also know it's never you. It's always your partner who gets it."

My temples tightened again; two screws being driven into the side of my head. "Suit yourself," I said.

I continued down the street towards the house. The place was well lit; an automobile was parked in front of the house. The lightning damaged oak loomed over me as I got closer. I didn't feel my temples anymore.

I climbed the steps to the small porch. I did notice my heartbeat had gone up. Was this the time that I got it, like Riley said? I thought about Joan and our unborn child. Were they going to go through life without a husband or a father? I grabbed the doorknob, twisted it and walked into the house.

The main room had two lamps burning brightly. There were no people in the room. The small bedroom had its door half open. There was a light on in there as well. I walked slowly towards this room, gun out in front of me. The only sound were my shoes walking as softly as I could. I stopped and then pushed the door in front of me all the way open.

What I saw made my heart leap. George Loftus, or what was left of him was tied tightly to the bed's four posts. He was not clothed. Every inch of him had been slashed by a very sharp knife. His body, the bed and the floor underneath it were saturated with blood. I felt dizzy for an instant and then threw up. When my stomach and head cleared, I looked at the woman in the chair at the foot of the bed.

Lucy VonMara was seated in the chair watching me. She was completely naked, her full body there for viewing. She was holding a six inch long knife. I could make out blood still dripping from it. "You men are all so weak."

I didn't say anything. I had no idea what she was talking about.

"Men like Loftus and Calvin Jessup. All they do is fall for the lust of a woman. They'll do anything for that woman, but they just don't ever realize when their time is up. There is a time when their usefulness is done. They never realize that. I tried to tell Loftus that, as sweet as he was, but he wouldn't listen. At least, dumb Calvin seemed to understand."

There was sweat running down my face; the room was very hot. "Why kill him?"

She laughed. "He wouldn't go away, Moses. He was like some faithful dog. He just wouldn't go and I had to leave town. I was going by myself. He wouldn't listen. Speaking of dogs, I see you met Calvin's."

I let my gun down to the side of my body. The dizziness was back. I was lightheaded. Seeing Loftus like that twisted me.

"I always dreamed of killing a cop, but one that was more a hero than Loftus. I dreamed of killing a cop like you, Detective Moses. I always felt a cop would kill me. I wanted to kill one of them before my time came." She got up from the chair and took a step towards me. I saw the magnificent body, but not the knife she still held. "Would you like to have me before I kill you, Detective?"

I didn't hear the commotion behind me, but I saw the look in her eyes, the realization that something was wrong. What I did hear was the roar of a .45 going off in my ear, not once but twice. The first slug caught her in the chest; the second hit her between the eyes, sending a good part of her head against the wall behind her. Her body tumbled to the floor.

"God damn it, Moses," Riley said. "God damn this fucking job!"

• • •

The longest day of my life had ended. I wasn't tired. I was so awake I was almost shaking. By the time we straightened up what had happened on 44th Street it was almost eight in the morning. The news of what had happened to Loftus had thrown the precinct into a quietness I had never seen. What had happened on 44th and what I'd seen with Father Corcoran had shocked me for the first time in my life. I'd have been dead by now if Riley hadn't followed me into that house. What had happened in the church on the southside seemed to have been years before. I thought I might be in shock.

Father Thomas Corcoran was charged with two counts of murder, Rebecca Tilson and Helen Gardner. The body of Rebecca Tilson was found and dug up exactly where Corcoran said it would be. I would be the only witness against him for what I had seen in the carriage barn. My testimony would lead him to the gallows. No one would need to report him to the Diocese.

George Loftus had fallen for Lucy VonMara and it had cost him his life. Not counting her frying of Horace Butross, Lucy had been rumored to be behind several murders. I'd never be able to prove any of these. The murder of Loftus was her work. I would never know who had shot young Carl Manning. I hoped it hadn't been Loftus. As for Lucy, there was no need for indictment or trial. Riley O'Donnell had provided all the justice anyone would ever need.

I was at my desk, looking over the reports I had written. We still had the unfinished business at the church fire. What would we learn? I shook my head and looked across the room at Riley. He was staring straight ahead and would occasionally take sips out of a bottle of whiskey on his desk. No one, including Shipley, would admonish him today. There was no doubt we had both seen Hell.

I was done and Riley was done for the day. The mess on the southside would have to wait. Those weren't murder victims anyway. They were casualties of war, a war that might just be getting underway. There wasn't one person responsible for this mess. It was a movement, sick as it was, to prove who was stronger or better. It was one of those things that would last forever, or longer, if that was possible. I got up to leave for home. I needed some rest. A runner came up from the lower level just as I got out of my chair. I had a visitor to see me.

● ● ●

I expected my visitor to be Sister Theresa. I had expected her to tell me that she knew Father Corcoran was a bad person all along. I was so wound up I was ready to agree with her about anything.

When I saw my visitors, I didn't know what to think. Sam Fuller was there with a little boy, chubby, maybe eight or nine years old. Sam looked forlorn, worn out. The kid had wide eyes. He looked frightened or shocked by the whole aspect of being in the police department. I pointed Sam to the one open meeting room. He took the young boy and led him in there. I followed and shut the door. I had no idea what to expect.

"I don't have any ideas about who might have started the fire last night. We were waiting for the morning to start asking around," I said.

"You don't have to ask around," Sam said.

The little kid was looking down at the floor; he had food that had spilled on his coat. "Do you want to explain?" I asked.

"This is William Jefferson, James' brother."

The boy didn't look up at the mention of his name.

"His mother didn't tell me, she was worried at the time that the killer might come looking for William, that William was there when his brother was hanged."

At first, I felt anger. The mother had withheld information that might have stopped a lot of this horror had she spoke up, but I saw her reasoning. "What did William see?"

Sam took a deep breath. "He saw the man that hung up James."

"William," I said. The boy looked up at me. "Did you really see this man?"

William nodded; tears started to run down his full face.

"That's not all," Sam said. "He was there last night by the church. He plays in those trees in the lot next door. He was up in one before the service started. He saw all of the people enter the church. When the service started, he saw the man tie the two doors shut and then start to light the bottles up and toss them through the windows. He saw the whole thing."

I knelt down and grabbed William lightly by the chin. He was looking at me, wide- eyed. "You saw it, William?"

He nodded. He was scared. "The same man?"

"Yes, sir," he spoke for the first time.

I turned to Sam Fuller. "Any idea who this man is?"

"This is my fault," he said. "I believed him. William saw this same man at that speech the Matthew Bartholomew gave. The man is the black man that works with Bartholomew. It is that man, Mr. Brand."

I felt my stomach drop. Mr. Brand, the heavy set, wide bodied man who looked like he had been stuffed into his suit. The man Bartholomew had introduced as his assistant. "You are sure about this?" I addressed this to Sam.

"Yes, sir," William said again. "My ma was afraid this man would come after me if I told anything."

Why would this man Brand murder a bunch of innocents, most of them the same color as him? Had he also caused the death of Whitey, the man beaten to behind The Taproom?

· · ·

"There is no doubt that Bartholomew and his crew arranged and carried out these murders to raise some sympathy for the blacks in the area. He was looking for donations to help his cause."

Lieutenant Shipley said this as we rolled along in a convoy of three vehicles to Bartholomew's office. I rode in the back of the lead auto with Shipley. The vehicle behind us held four cops. The last vehicle, following as quickly as it could, was a horse drawn van.

"He wanted people to feel bad and drop money into his coffers to help him fight his cause, which we now know was a complete ruse. If anything, the man is a consummate con artist."

I couldn't disagree. I had never seen Shipley this animated. After I told him what Sam Fuller had said he had insisted that he be along for the arrests; I went to get Riley, but it seemed his little whiskey sips had gotten the best of him.

"What's the plan once we get there?" I asked. Shipley hadn't been in the field for a while and what we were going to do was a little risky; I wasn't sure the man known as Mr. Brand would come along that easily. We did have six police officers, all armed, with us. That didn't mean there couldn't be violence.

We pulled up in front of Bartholomew's office on Wabash at a little past ten. It was starting to rain and the wind had picked up; one of the city's elevated cars rumbled above us on the tracks. We all got out of our vehicles and approached the office. Shipley stopped before we went in.

"Moses and I will lead the way. All weapons drawn. This could be a dangerous situation," Shipley said.

I was worried, but then I wondered if there would actually be a shootout in an office in the Loop. Shipley started for the door to the place. I drew my gun.

"Good morning, gentlemen," a young, smiling receptionist said to us as we came through the door. I held my badge up high for her to see it. She swallowed hard.

"Mr. Bartholomew," I said.

Shipley pointed towards the back of the place. I could see Bartholomew and his aides in a small, glass enclosed room. Shipley headed in that direction. We left the poor receptionist with her mouth hanging open.

Shipley moved quickly to the room the men were in. He didn't stop. He pushed the door open and walked right in. Bartholomew didn't look upset or concerned. He stopped the speech he was giving to Mr. Brand and Mr. Jenkins and looked up at Shipley. "Good morning, Lieutenant."

"Cut the nonsense," Shipley said. "We have reason to believe that you and your people are responsible for several of the murders on the southside in an effort to cause a sympathetic reaction to help raise money for your little enterprise."

Bartholomew and Mr. Brand smiled. "That is the most preposterous accusation and statement that I have ever heard," Bartholomew said.

"We also have an eyewitness who saw Mr. Brand hang James Jefferson and also bind the doors and ignite the fire at the church last night. The three of you are under arrest for murder."

Brand came out of his chair quicky but thought twice as he looked into the barrel of my revolver.

"Again, an absolute astonishing accusation," Bartholomew said. "One that my lawyer will clear up in minutes with a call to the mayor."

"Stop," the little secretary Jenkins said loudly. "Stop all of this lying. This has gone too far. It was supposed to be once or twice, not go on like this."

"Shut up, Mr. Jenkins," Bartholomew said.

Tears started to stream down the face of Jenkins. "Too many deaths," he said. "Too many and kids and old people, too. Too much."

Shipley exhaled deeply. "You will be escorted to the Central Station from here where you will be booked. You may contact your lawyer then. For the time being, I suggest that you come along quietly. I would hate for Detective Moses to have to shoot one of you. Sometimes his antics get under my skin a bit, but if he was forced to use his weapon, I would have no problem condoning it."

• • •

When I returned to the precinct and took a seat at my desk, I thought I would be relaxed. Instead I found myself as tense as I ever recall feeling. Muscles in my neck, head and shoulders tightened. I wanted to talk with someone, but I was alone. Riley had retreated to his house, apparently rather drunk. Shipley had stayed on at the Central Station. The second floor was quiet and my mind was racing.

I was sure that Father Corcoran and Robert had tortured and murdered two young girls. Were there others and how many more would there be if they had not been stopped. Maybe we could find an answer to the first part; the second part was unanswerable.

We might be able to prove that Lucy VonMara had killed a prostitute after Calvin Jessup had left a second story door open for her. Other than that, the other prostitutes or clients who had allegedly died by her hands would never be proved. The one that stung was Loftus; he had been drawn in by Lucy and had paid the ultimate price for his obsession. I knew George Loftus as well as I'd known anyone on the force. I would never understand what had happened to him.

The tale of Matthew Bartholomew was a sick and confusing one. He had started his Chicago Negro League to help the newly arriving blacks in the area, a good thing. He had then used his heavy, Mr. Brand, to set up the Irish community as the bad guy by killing a number of blacks. I wasn't sure of the exact total from the church fire, but I had counted close to fifteen deaths in all. Bartholomew and his friends deserved nothing less than the noose.

I knew if I went back to my apartment I would get a full grilling from Joan. I was not ready for that. I had been awake for over twenty-four hours, but I was nowhere near sleep. The only thing that made sense was Cooper's and a glass of whiskey.

It was too early for Kenny, the usual bartender to be in, but Joey would suffice. I had met him before. He was a chatty sort and the bar wasn't that crowded. We talked a lot about nothing. The whiskey flowed easily. I found myself getting drunk and at some point I felt a little numb. I remembered thinking that a visit to Soon Lee's opium den might be what I needed. I remember clearly thinking about that, but that is about all I remember. After that, I recall nothing.

Chapter Thirteen

When I woke up, I was in a room that I didn't recognize. My shoulders and back ached. My mouth was as dry as a desert. I rolled over in the bed that I was sleeping in. I looked around. The room had one window that showed sunlight coming through it. One the wall on one side was a picture of Christ; above the bed hung a crucifix. I had been in this room before.

I sat up on the bed as the door to my left opened. Sister Theresa entered the room and smiled at me. "I see you have returned to the living, Detective Moses."

"This is the orphanage," I said.

"Yes, it is," she said. "We actually put you in Father Luigi's old room."

I rubbed my eyes. "How did I get here?"

She came around the side of the bed and looked at me. "You don't remember?"

"I wouldn't ask you that question if I remembered."

She smiled again. "We found you on the front steps. You were lying across one of them. There was an empty bottle of whiskey at the bottom of the stairs. We assumed you had consumed it because we couldn't wake you. You were completely in another world."

I remembered Cooper's, that was it. "How long ago?"

"You have been in this room two days. You have slept for two days."

Two days, I thought. Out of commission for two whole days. I thought of Joan. "No one asked about me?"

"Not to my knowledge."

"I've got to get home."

"Your clothes and coat have been cleaned. They are hanging in the closet."

"I suppose I should thank you."

She laughed. "You never appeared to be in any real danger. You were just out, snoring loudly."

I nodded. "I have to go."

When I got out of the bed, it felt like every muscle and bone in my body ached. It took a while to get dressed. When I got outside into the cold, it was another wait to track down a carriage. I told the driver to get to my apartment as quickly as possible. The horse seemed to have other ideas. It seemed to plod along.

I bound up the stairs to our place, taking two steps at a time. I was dreading the meeting at the top of them. When I got to our apartment, I found the door closed, but unlocked. I rushed into the apartment. I could only see the main room and the kitchen area. Joan was not in either of these. I moved into the bedroom. The bed was completely made. I checked the closet first and then the dresser by the window. My clothes were present in both of these. Joan's were gone. She was gone.

I stepped back into the living room and sat in my favorite chair. Three old *Tribunes* were on the table by it. In all of my selfish behavior I had forgotten the most important thing in my life. I was alone again. I had no idea where she had gone. I rubbed the stubble on my face. I felt twenty years older.

"Moses, you okay?"

I looked up and Riley O'Donnell was in the door that I had left open. "I think so. Joan is gone."

"We were looking all over for you. The people at Cooper's had seen you, but that was where the leads ended."

"I had a bit of a bad time," I said. "I came home and found out Joan has left me."

Riley nodded his head. "I'm sorry to hear that, Moses. She seemed like a sweet girl."

"Yeah," I said.

"Anyway, Shipley told me to run by here and see if you showed up."

"Shipley," I said.

"Yes. Lieutenant Shipley."

"What does he want?"

"Moses, there has been a murder down in the Levee. Shipley wants us to handle it."

I looked around the vacant apartment one more time. I got up slowly and followed Riley down the stairs to the waiting vehicle.

The End

About the Author

John Sturgeon is the author of the four-book *Levee District* series published by Black Rose Writing. Black Rose has also published his stand alone novel, *The Murder of Fatty Fuller*. John is an avid reader and mediocre golfer. He resides in Wheaton, Illinois and his winter residence in Sarasota, Florida, with his wife, Mary.

Note from the Author

Word-of-mouth is crucial for any author to succeed. If you enjoyed *Evil Returns*, please leave a review online—anywhere you are able. Even if it's just a sentence or two. It would make all the difference and would be very much appreciated.

Thanks!
John Sturgeon

We hope you enjoyed reading this title from:

BLACK ROSE
writing™

www.blackrosewriting.com

Subscribe to our mailing list – *The Rosevine* – and receive **FREE** books, daily deals, and stay current with news about upcoming releases and our hottest authors.
Scan the QR code below to sign up.

Already a subscriber? Please accept a sincere thank you for being a fan of Black Rose Writing authors.

View other Black Rose Writing titles at
www.blackrosewriting.com/books and use promo code
PRINT to receive a **20% discount** when purchasing.